Women

I

Know

Women

I

Know

Katerina Gibson

SCRIBNER

SCRIBNER

First published in Australia in 2022 by Scribner, an imprint of Simon & Schuster Australia
Suite 19A, Level 1, Building C, 450 Miller Street, Cammeray, NSW 2062

Sydney New York London Toronto New Delhi
Visit our website at www.simonandschuster.com.au

SCRIBNER and design are registered trademarks of The Gale Group, Inc.,
used under licence by Simon & Schuster Inc.

10 9 8 7 6 5 4 3 2 1

A catalogue record for this
book is available from the
National Library of Australia

9781761106811 (paperback)
9781761106828 (ebook)

Artwork on p. 6 supplied courtesy of Jenny Odell.
Extract from *Vertigo* by W. G. Sebald, published by Vintage on p. vii, copyright © 1990,
Vito von Eichborn Verlag, Frankfurt am Main. English language translation copyright
© 1999, Michael Hulse. Reprinted with permission of The Random House Group Limited.
Cover design by Alissa Dinallo
Cover image by Rozenn Le Gall
Typeset by Midland Typesetters in 12.5/17 pt Adobe Garamond Pro
Printed and bound in Australia by Griffin Press

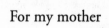

For my mother

I walked to the edge of the road, and knew that I had never gazed down into such chasms before.

– *Vertigo,* W.G. Sebald

Contents

Glitches in The Algorithm

When I first started work on The Algorithm I'd wake, with the help of an app, to the sound of chirping at the precise moment that the sun rose over the horizon and *ombre*-d my bedroom in peaches. Next, I'd pick up my phone, search for smoothies in the muddy-green spectrum—kale, coconut milk, spinach, bananas—put on a playlist, either Morning Vibes or Pop n Fresh, pair my headphones, turn them to silent, and then fall asleep for two more hours. On my second waking, I'd brew a coffee, pour a glass of water, and roll a cigarette that I smoked through the kitchen window, while, with my location off, I looked up bus times to the gym where I paid seven dollars a week—a membership I signed up for in a fit of optimism before my work on The Algorithm began. While I can only imagine this gym being filled with wide-shouldered men of myriad sweat patterns and foreheads crumpled to varying wrinkle depths (puzzled bewilderment on the sit-up machine, concerned knot between the eyes at the bench press, crevasse-like worrying at their own form in the mirror), this small expense ultimately came to benefit the overall path of The Algorithm.

I'd stub out my cigarette, take a shit, pour the glass of water into whichever plant looked the thirstiest, and then leave the house to catch the 8:46 to work. While on the train I'd put on Workout Beats that I'd then spend the journey considering; in the morning commute claustrophobia the music to me did not seem made for human consumption, but a robotic rave, glitching and looping as if incidental, computer-generated.

From the train station to work I'd scroll and tap indiscriminately, without looking down, letting The Algorithm do the work for me, a method that always resulted—whenever I checked my likes during work hours—in a pictorial spread of cocktail parties, bikini pictures, sunsets, selfies in geometrically intricate sunglasses, and aerial shots of aesthetic cheese platters. Over time, as my work on The Algorithm progressed, this content shifted to include pictures of engagement rings, dogs, babies, small children better dressed than me. Not all at once, but gradually, as She—my algorithmic self—became, in my mind, more maternal. But as I say, that came later, as my idea of Her evolved; phase one of my work stayed grounded in emulating socialites and fashion students. I walked and scrolled and double-tapped. There was a nice rhythm to this that gave me a satisfaction, a meditation for the day ahead.

Throughout my work hours I'd keep my location securely off. Although, even shoved into the bowels of my bag, my phone caught snippets of my conversation. I worked at an outgoing call centre, conducting a government survey that started as a 'proactive response' to the protestors that now took to the streets most weeks. It was hard to eliminate this aspect of my life from The Algorithm. I tried leaving my phone in another part of the office, 'forgot' it on a charger in the kitchen, but then I was exposing it to the element of rogue and gossipy co-workers, whose conversations I could not control and which often involved confidential survey answers. It simply never crossed my mind to turn it off. As consequence, I had trouble recalibrating Her in the eyes of The Algorithm, politically speaking. At first this didn't concern me, or didn't really occur to me. Truthfully, at that point I didn't know what I was doing, or I'd convinced myself I didn't know. In what I now see as the beginning stages of my work on The Algorithm, self-deception was the defining feature.

A denial: when I first started my work, I did so because I really thought I *would* go to the gym. That *this* week I would not let vegetables in my crisper rot. That listening to workout music was just one step away from actually working out, and et cetera. I believed then that I would catch up to the algorithmic self I was putting out in the world. That I was simply researching the possibilities of my day before selecting a different future. I didn't realise then what I was doing—I was making art.

After work I'd catch the train home, headphones on with nothing playing, watching my reflection in the window while it resolved and unresolved itself as the train passed through tunnels, by large dark buildings. From my station I would walk to the bottle shop where I'd purchase a flask-sized bottle of whiskey. Occasionally, if I had the money and the mood hit me, I'd go to Best Chinese Takeaway next door and buy sweet and sour pork or stir-fried noodles. All these types of purchases—takeaway, alcohol, cigarettes—I bought with cash, out of two crisp hundred-dollar notes I withdrew from the ATM at the start of every week; I later labelled these in my banking app 'Brunch and Coffee'.

I would then walk myself and my dinner, liquid or solid, to the park, where I'd sit atop the hill as the sun appeared to grow larger approaching the horizon, and watch the scene below. Joggers of neon-striped shoes swept up and down the river, swerving strolling families and other neon-clad men on bikes and men on bikes with megaphones, themselves conducting the rowers gliding along the river behind them, themselves, the rowers, swerved by the black swans making their daily pilgrimage up the Maribyrnong to nibble on stonewort at the water's edge. On the bank, tan border collies chased smaller dogs of evident psychological issue; large African, Asian and Caucasian families of complex structures barbecued; in the playground children swung and leaped, leaped and swung, heedless of their growing bones; and closest to myself, in the shadow of ginkgo trees, young couples in near copulation lay oblivious to the children, dogs, swans, and et cetera.

While I watched this I would sit almost completely still, only raising my flask or chopsticks to my mouth, and—perhaps because of a combination of this stillness and my vantage point on the hill that miniaturised the people below, making them appear like intricate figurines—feel that I was outside time. Or rather that I was participating in it differently. The toing and froing of the scene below brought on vertiginous time: on a molecular level I was aware of the sensation of time passing faster at my heightened position; the emptiness of my mind allowed my body to experience a scientific phenomenon that would usually take the stature of a Himalayan Mountain—as opposed to the steady incline of Footscray Park hill—to observe. Although this, on reflection, sounds dangerously hippyish. Much more likely, I was simply experiencing a prolonged form of dissociation.

Whatever the cause of this feeling, it would inevitably end as the pedestrians thinned, picnic blankets were shaken out, rowers returned their boats to the boatshed, and dogs and children were—with difficultly—extracted from the park. As the people dissipated and the scene below quickened, clicked back into natural time, I was left disappointed. The park in its emptiness a blank canvas; it was the people and movement that interested me. There's a series of artworks I saw online once called *All the People on Google Earth,* satellite images of places with all but the people removed. This was during a time when I still did things like seek out art, and perhaps because it was one of the last pieces of art I consensually experienced since beginning work on The Algorithm—before I began working on my own art—I've found myself at times mentally removing the non-human elements of a scene, trying to see people interacting with one another sans context. And so, when, on my hill, the people emptied the scene below, I'd be left in acute isolation—alone, in a blank space. In the next moment, re-entering time and place, the scene before me resolved itself: I was a woman alone in a park at night, and I would then leave.

When I got home I'd scroll through videos of pus being exhumed—a fringe consequence for those who aspired to pure beautification, difficult to iron out, the dark side of The Algorithm's moon—ribbons of discharge shooting out of unsuspecting blackheads, or squelching continuously from horrific pits, interrupted sometimes with the before-and-after of a nose job or lip injection gone awry. I would scroll for hours until I was at least as disgusted by the content as I was in myself, then masturbate and fall asleep.

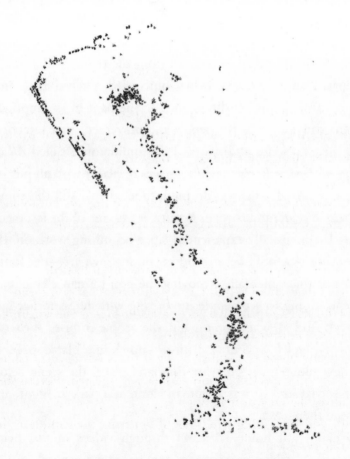

All the People in on Pier 39, Jenny Odell

I'm not sure entirely when the second stage of my work on The Algorithm began. Where it is that the delineating line between the first and second phase can be drawn, when I realised what I was doing.

It would be simple to retroactively ascribe a single moment, an epiphany. Perhaps it was watching my face superimposed on a scene through the train window one afternoon. I could say that when the train entered a tunnel, the window a mirror, I 'saw' myself, came into a sudden moment of awareness.

But the truth is, the second stage of my work on The Algorithm began gradually, as I began to go off script.

Have you or members of your immediate family been affected by unprecedented weather events caused by the seasonal weather depression of El Niño and/or local arsonists?
Pardon?
If so, have you or any members of your immediate family been relocated, temporarily evacuated or removed in situ?
I—yes.
Relocated, temporarily evacuated, or removed in situ?
We lived in a school gym for a week if that's what you mean.
Were the services provided adequate and/or was the accommodation you returned to fit for living?
I mean, my house was still standing if that's what you're asking. But everything was ruined and—I mean *no,* the gym was crowded and unregulated, a woman was—
Thank you for taking time out of your day to complete this valuable survey.
Wait! [. . .]

Have you or members of your immediate family been affected by unprecedented weather events caused by the seasonal weather depression of El Niño and/or local arsonists?
Oh fuck you [. . .]

Have you or members of your immediate family been affected by unprecedented weather events caused by the seasonal weather depression of El Niño and/or local arsonists?
Funny way of saying climate change.
A mental loop-the-loop if there ever was one.
Pardon?
Yes or no?
I—Yes, Jesus.
If so, have you or any members of your immediate family been relocated, temporarily evacuated or removed in situ?
We've been relocated. What does 'removed in situ' mean? Rescued? Relocated after being rescued?
Were the services provided adequate and/or was the accommodation you were relocated to fit for living?
No. What's your name, hon, how did you end up with this job?
What aspects of your relocation did you find inadequate?
Everything, to put it mildly. I know a lot of people were doing the best in a bad situation, we were stuck on a boat for days, and then my daughter caught a cold that didn't get treated and now she's wheezing when she sleeps. The place we're in now? Previous occupants are still hanging around: rats, everywhere. Everything that has gone right—meals, extra clothes and blankets,

chargers—that's been down to the people here. The community, nothing to do with the government.

Thank you for taking time out of your day to complete this valuable survey.

God love, I hope you find a more fulfil [. . .]

Have you or members of your immediate family been affected by unprecedented weather events caused by the seasonal weather depression of El Niño and/or local arsonists?

Mum! [. . .]

Have you or members of your immediate family been affected by unprecedented weather events caused by the seasonal weather depression of El Niño and/or local arsonists?

Who did you say this is?

If so, have you or any members of your immediate family been relocated, temporarily evacuated or removed in situ?

I mean, obviously yeah. You know where you're calling, right?

No, actually.

What?

Not the foggiest, where are you?

What?

Thank you for your time.

[. . .]

Have you or members of your immediate family been affected by unprecedented weather events caused by the seasonal weather depression of El Niño and/or local arsonists?

Are you fucking kidding me mate? [. . .]

9

Have you or members of your immediate family been affected by unprecedented weather events caused by the seasonal weather depression of El Niño and/or local arsonists?

How can something be both seasonal and unprecedented? Hello?

[. . .]

Have you or members of your immediate family been affected by recent events?

Yup.

If so, have you or any members of your immediate family been relocated, temporarily evacuated or removed in situ?

We were evacuated. We were meant to be relocated, but I couldn't do it. They wanted to take us up north. Up *closer* to the tropics. Maniacs.

Were the services provided adequate and/or was the accommodation you were relocated to fit for living?

You're a riot, aren't you. What was I just saying? Fucking terrible, obviously. And the way people act when this shit happens. No fucking humanity, everyone for themselves. People would step over their own grandmother. I'm camping in my yard—not one of the neighbours has even stopped by to see if we're alive. We have a kid, mind you, although he's gone to his grandparents with his mother now. And my dog, Benji, gone. In the thick of it all. Just fucked off into the bush. I thought maybe he just got lost, confused. He's pretty good at looking after himself, but still, he should be back by now.

Jesus Christ.

What?

Sorry about your dog.

Thanks love—you're just about the only person who is.

You never know, he might come back.

[*Sigh*] I don't reckon.

Thank you for taking the time out of your day to complete this valuable survey.

[. . .]

Have you or members of your immediate family been affected by recent events?

Who hasn't?

Sorry, um . . . If so, have you or any of your family had to move?

You're calling us on our home phone, aren't you? So yeah, we're fine, but I reckon we're the only ones who are, really.

Oh that's good. Is your dog okay?

What?

Just call me curious.

Yeah, our dog is—how did you know we had a dog?

Thanks for completing this valuable survey.

[. . .]

Hello. This call is to check on the status of the residents of this address.

Mary?

You are not in any immediate danger?

Yeah—no. I mean, it was scary, but we're okay. Very lucky—who's this?

You have supplies and access to water?
Um, yeah. Well, at least for now we do.
And you're—is your day going well?
What the fuck is happening?
Thank you for your time.
[. . .]

No matter what I did outside work hours to digitally carve a picture of Her, as long as I stuck even somewhat to the script at work, the outside world refracted itself back into The Algorithm. In between svelte blondes in bikinis and raised glasses of Aperol spritz distorting sunsets, there'd be links to articles about the latest calamity, with detailed explanations of why Shell or Gina Rinehart or Jeff Bezos was to blame, profiles on cleared land masses, bleached coral, prolific protestors, all of which on my walk to work I would inadvertently tap, causing similar content to reoccur. It wasn't that I didn't want The Algorithm to imagine Her as generous, but I certainly didn't want Her to be genuinely socially and environmentally conscious—too much of a downer. The trajectory of The Algorithm was giving her a feedback loop of social consciousness that fed into cynicism that fed into genuine learning that fed into deeper social consciousness, and et cetera. I did not want her to appear enlightened, intellectually. For instance, it was okay for The Algorithm to think she'd like heart-warming footage of wombats being saved, but if it went as far as to suggest she'd be interested in how the government had failed to protect the wombats in the first place, then She needed recalibration.

Throughout stage two, I began to take more cognisant steps towards making Her unsullied by the real me. I started to actually go to the gym. Not to work out, but I would stand outside the building and attend to my social media more presently. I shared touched-up photos of me from years ago in tight, high-waisted jean shorts. I purchased the latest trending self-help book and quoted large chunks without reading it. On the way home from work, I started listening to podcasts with breathing exercises. I still drank heavily in the park, but not as often. I stopped masturbating after watching videos of cysts being popped, and started inviting over boys I met on Tinder who owned Labradors and wore chinos the same colour as their Labradors. These biblically named men—Jacobs, or Davids, or Matthews, or Josephs— would come and give me a rigorous but unsatisfying rut. I would sometimes let a Nathaniel or a Daniel hang around for a few days and buy me expensive Instagrammable dinners. If they were in good enough shape, I would let them appear in the background. On these dates, I would let Her order two bottles of white and giggle and overshare, inserting faux childhood memories: why my father didn't love me, the deep competitive complex with my sister, why I was scared of cats. Sometimes I surprised myself by sharing real memories, letting my true self slip out and animate Her. I would tell Liam about the time I went camping as a child near a river when the rope swing snapped over a rock, then trace the thin scar that circled my elbow and crept up to my pinkie, or I would regale Caleb with descriptions of my childhood attic room, the mould, the pneumonia, and the reason my voice rang two octaves down from my peers. Sometimes these men surprised me by telling me how much they loved their mother, and later, giving me an orgasm. But most of the time I told them the scar was from an abusive former boyfriend, or a hiking trip, I'd leave my Scarlett-Johansson-turned-coal miner voice a mystery, and the sex remained anticlimactic.

And it worked: as I began to go more gradually off script; as I unfollowed socialites, and started following recently pregnant mothers who did not look as if they'd been recently pregnant with hobbies like ceramics, baking oatmeal cookies, and wearing organic linen; as I started commenting on high-school friends' engagements with pink-heart exclamation points; as I actually purchased the ingredients for my smoothies; as I, throughout the day, shook my phone vigorously enough to get to ten thousand steps, I started getting ads for crystals and organic baby food. Centrist, non-threatening politicians kept popping up in my feed. Nothing experimental music-wise came up on Spotify. Instead of talks by upcoming, politically relevant essay writers, I was invited to events like Bottomless Cocktails at The Docklands. I didn't go but I clicked 'attending'. I purchased, or at least put in my cart, various items The Algorithm dictated She liked, and slowly filled my house with skincare products I am too scared to use, shoes I don't have the agility to wear, and kitchen utensils of function I am uncertain.

I wasn't actually losing weight or exhaling deeply through my nose on my commutes. To actually walk that much or eat my greens would be too dangerously close to self-improvement, and my aim wasn't to self-improve, it was to leave a pretty digital corpse.

A stroke of genius came when I downloaded a period-tracking app, and gave Her a start-of-the-month, three-day light bleed with symptoms like 'minor cramps' and 'increased sex drive', where in reality I would start bleeding each month as the moon disappeared in the sky. On nights when I went to the hill and the sun set—not into a gentle illumination of the newly solid landscape, but into a dark void that mirrored the white void in my imagined *All the People of Footscray Park*—I would feel the foreboding gravitational shift of an impending five-day flow, and the contextualisation of last week's suicidal thoughts.

I smoothed out the problem of my job informing The Algorithm, and in turn informing Her, by replacing the mandated questions on my survey with small talk that sometimes resulted in surprisingly long conversations with strangers. I talked about their niece's star sign, their bird's diet, communism, socialism, capitalism, and variously why these systems were alike or unlike. I talked about toothpaste brands and dentist costs and puppies, and sons and daughters and wives and husbands, and why these sons and daughters and especially husbands didn't love them, and rose gardens and beetroot crops. I talked about traffic congestion and why this was or wasn't the government's fault. I listened to stories of pride and conquest and triumph. I occasionally listened to homophobic or racist or transphobic or misogynist tirades that I hung up on or stayed completely silent on the other end of, or even, occasionally, questioned the pontificator of, which would then make said pontificator defensive or silent—in anger or shock I could not say. I listened to complaints and encouragements regarding the protestors. I heard about people's malfunctioning washing machines and internet, and jobs and lives. We rarely talked about why I had called, or why they were not themselves too busy to take this call, or what exactly the protesters were protesting, and this suited me, suited Her, just fine.

By this time, I had started to conceptualise Her as a want-to-be mother. I barely had time to go down to the river, and had to drink my whiskey while researching baby names, downloading fertility apps and reading deep, contradictory passages in long-abandoned forums on the joys and pains of childbirth. I sat in my kitchen, blue glow of my screen illuminating me in shirt, underwear, one foot resting under my ass, and craved moments of decontextualisation, where I would be just a person in my void, hovering in the air, imagining my neighbour downstairs taking a piss, the tinkling of the liquid hitting porcelain silenced, the stream disappearing mid-flow.

Then I was fired. It should have happened sooner, but because of the size of the call centre and the work ethic of our alleged management, it took several months for me to be called into my supervisor's office to have the following conversation:

Supervisor: Pearl, what did I just listen to?

Me: Beg your pardon?

Supervisor: The conversation about rehabilitating a garden with the elderly lady in Gippsland.

Me: Yes.

Supervisor: That went for thirty minutes?

Me: Some people are very thorough with their answers.

Supervisor: Where you discuss a recipe for a cucumber face mask for ten minutes.

Me: Ah.

Supervisor: I've had to go through your call log, Pearl, your job is to—

Me [trying to hide my phone]: Shhhh!

Supervisor:
Me: I'll go then.
Supervisor: That would be best.

After my firing, instead of feeling intense anxiety at my impending empty bank account, I felt the last tether to my real self dissipate. I saw ahead no kinks or setbacks in The Algorithm, but only Her.

Liberated, finally, from the struggles of others, my work began in earnest and I—no, how about this—and She flourished. And thus stage three began. She woke in the morning to a gentle trill, She drank water and smoked a cigarette, but had the shame to dispense of the butt and douse the kitchen in an artificial floral odour afterwards. She caught the train not into work, but still into the city, and without worrying about turning Her location off, or the urgency of the people walking behind Her, pottered through the streets and alleyways, through shopping centres, in and out of boutiques and nurseries, and ordered excessive lattes in laneway cafes, all the while humming in content, caressing Her stomach in what She imagined was an expectant way. On hot days She went to bars and ordered lemon-lime bitters that I'd slip whiskey into when the waiter was preoccupied, and browsed appropriately sanguine magazines while wearing ornate floppy hats. Or She had Caleb drive Her to the beach and photograph Her. And this worked too: people assumed Her stomach was swollen in the foetal—as opposed to sweet and sour pork, and whiskey—way; She would catch snippets of strangers proclaiming She had a pregnant glow, smiling in Her direction. Caleb fled, but other Tinder boys remained.

During this time I ran out of money, and She, in the most natural progression possible, began to wander into boutique stores and make odd requests, stealing socks and lipsticks and eventually money. I am not sure if it was me or Her really. She would request a children's woollen hat in a different size and colour, I would find the right button on the computer and the drawer would open. Security in the average retail store is phenomenally lax. During this moment, after the shopkeeper left and I slid open the till, slipped myself one hundred, two hundred bucks and pushed it shut again, the world would tighten then disappear, and we would watch ourselves, Her and me, as the wall to the storage room, the desk, the windows, dissolved and we could see through to the shop clerk rummaging through nothing, or checking their phone, and we would watch people passing in what was just previously the street outside. In this moment we craved, without the world (*All the People in/around Shop 49*), I would tuck the money into my jacket pocket, then the shop assistant would come back, frowning in apology, and I would wave her off like it was nothing and leave. As I turned, racks of lunchboxes, or novelty socks, or lotions, or cards reasserted their existence in my periphery, ornate doorframes uncoiled themselves back into position, cobble stones from the street outside rose up solid to meet my feet.

And this is how She went on, as long as we took only a little, went to disparate parts of the city, surrounding suburbs, changing hairstyles and glasses. This worked for Her too, in The Algorithm. She was a whimsical traveller; I could capture moments all over the city in cute cafes and hidden beaches. Even if someone was to suspect us, the police were too busy with the almost daily protestors to care about a petty thief. We walked, we stole, we lived in moments of compression when the world dissolved and we were one person, milling among others, watching people navigate the non-city.

In this lifestyle She was sustainable. I had finally tweaked Her enough, removed the caustic parts of myself that were making the data replicate me in digital space. I do not mean to be trite when I say that it worked in the way that I had wanted, and that in my art I had made Her so convincing that The Algorithm no longer attempted to cater to me, but to Her, and I became Her—or at least more like Her. The film that separated us dissolved, which isn't to say that I became more authentic, but rather that I had made another self that I could, without irony or self-loathing, be. More simplistically, I had removed my knowledge of the world from Her, and in inhabiting Her, was able to inhabit the world.

She was on the ground floor of a multi-level fast-fashion place in the city centre. The teenage shop attendant went to find a different-size blouse, remarking on the protestors passing, rain-drenched, outside.

'You'd just be *miserable.*'

I said yes, they must be, instead of encouraging him to imagine the level of discontent the protesters must have to keep doing what they were doing. At that moment I realised that even if I'd wanted to say anything on behalf of the protesters' cause, I couldn't. Her unknowing had become my own. I slipped my hand behind the till and plucked two hundred dollars, having a brief prophetical flash of this young man being fired. But nothing happened. Nothing disappeared as it usually did in the grace period after stealing where my heart beat in paradiddles and the world vanished. Everything stayed solid. My heart beat on steadily. I could not imagine the teenager standing in some back corner, and instead saw—could only see—the door to the backroom, the counter beneath my elbows. Without calling out, I slipped myself out into streets, and was so immediately absorbed by the murmuring and chanting and shifting of the protesters it seemed to happen even before the wet and rush of rain hit me, and continued to hit me, my hair quickly becoming heavy with water.

Stopped cars beeped quick excited honks of encouragement, or long aggressive ones in annoyance. Windscreen wipers whipped back and forth revealing tired people with their heads leant back, children with hands pressed up to the glass. Some people, in complete defeat, left their wipers off, the rain let to make a curtain of privacy. I soaked through to my undershirt in minutes, and my socks soon followed. As we marched, I tried to disappear us into blank space, to imagine the long tail of people sans context, thousands of us walking together through the void. I attempted to imagine our voices not reverberating off the tall buildings, amplifying as they bounced back, but instead dissipating into nothing as soon as they left our throats. I began to shiver and tried to picture the person next to me tripping over nothing, not the root of a plane tree breaching the bitumen, all of us wet not from the rain, but as if of our own accord. I tried to imagine the world disintegrating, leaving us, a disembodied crowd, cornering our way around the non-city, a game of snake with nothing to eat, *All the People On*, *All the People In*, bodies replicating data in white space. I looked around at the stubborn environment, the pavement, the bus stops, the trees, the gutter, the smell, the light and colour, the rain puddling and streaming down the side of buildings, coruscant.

Meat Alternatives for the Motherland: A Review

ARTICHOKE 'FISH': You meet again at a restaurant that serves artichoke broiled and seasoned to taste, feel, smell, exactly like fish. She will not be intimate with a meat eater she says, leaving the impression of her lips in orange on the rim of her wineglass. Outside: the sound of car tyres slicing through water, the glint of light rearranging itself on the asphalt as the puddles settle. Your saliva glands are in overdrive. She looks, in some green wrap-around complexly secured, her hair piled up, black eyes without apparent irises, beautiful. Starting this story is simple.

JIM'S SHREDDED 'CHICKEN': Paired with vegan mayo, secured between lettuce and wholemeal bread, between Tupperware lid and bottom, in a backpack through which your arms are slipped, those same arms steering a bike as you ride down a footpath adjacent to a river. In front of you: her. When she turns to talk her words are lost in the wind, her helmet slaps low-hanging

22

wattle, sending puffs of yellow pollen to engulf you. You sneeze, she laughs, and this at least, her laugh, cannot be appropriated by the wind—high and clear, like bells ringing. Everything tastes like chicken.

100% DAIRY-FREE MOZZARELLA-STYLE BLOCK: You stay up far into the am watching black and white films on the projector. Fellini, Bergman. You pull homemade pizza out of the oven and eat on the couch, your legs entwined in the bliss of a peaceful month. The doorbell rings.

ROAST VEGETABLES: Old-fashioned greens and potato will have to do. She reminds her mother that fish is not vegetarian. Pink salmon belly glistens on the kitchen bench. A pointy grey cat is pawing a corner of butchers paper hanging off the bench, the salmon on top it inching towards the edge. The cat's devotion to its master narrative is comical, and you laugh. So April, her mother says, pouring you a large glass of white wine so clear it could be water, what do you do with yourself?

EGGLESS PASTA IN THE DARK: On your anniversary the power goes out. You find enough candles to illuminate the kitchen in a shimmer; the feast you planned will not be defeated. It's like fancy camping, you say as you grill zucchini on the gas stove, feed dough through the pasta maker, very fancy camping. You can see the outline of her on the couch but she does not respond. The candles' lights are doubled in the window. All at once the dots of fire in the reflection begin to move, lifting off from the laws of physics like fireflies. Tingles shudder through your limbs in waves. Holy shit, you say, quick, look at this. The shadow on the couch does not move. There is only silence, and then a slow, tired sigh.

'TUNA' HORS D'OEUVRES: Amazing, you say, slipping the dry biscuits topped with sauce topped with 'tuna' topped with dill into your mouth—all of it, you have been assured, is vegan. All at once the ingredients dissipate over your tongue. She narrows her eyes. You repeat what the waiter told you. In the monopolising blackness of her irises, there's the room, tiny, inverted: people in long dresses and fashionable mules and dangly earrings that catch and flicker the light; teenagers in black carrying trays of hors d'oeuvres, flutes of champagne that are probably techni-cally sparkling wine; old men holding jackets folded over their arm, young men holding jackets just the same, and you, fish-eyed in the middle, caught mid-chew, cheek bulging, contorting the rest of the scene to the edges. You fix your expression and swallow. You see in her eyes one of the artists—the friend whose work you have come to see—coming towards you, the sound of their clicking heels echoing though the ravine of the gallery. Her expression snaps to a smile, and you turn to greet your friend. They frown and ask if everything is okay. Later while leaving you say, what the fuck was that? and she says, you shouldn't trust people so much. Again you say, what the fuck was that? and that night she doesn't touch you.

MARINATED TOFU: A simple, cheap, wholesome alternative that can be easily prepared and used in your day-to-day cooking, with noodles, rice-paper rolls, curry, stir-fries. This is not what your neighbour is thinking as he watches you through your kitchen window from his balcony, glancing from the pan to your uncovered chest, her hanging off your neck like a dependent marsupial.

AFTER-FLESH BACON STRIPS: Her head on your lap, her chest rising in quick compressions, tears streaming sideways elongating her eyeliner, feline. Her hair is splayed and knotted. On the stove strips of processed soy lie forgotten in the pan. But they don't blacken and harden, setting off the smoke alarm as they should. Instead they congeal into a strange sinewy tangle, looking, as you clean them off the pan, like knotted heartstrings.

MUESLI BARS: Your jaw is not used to chewing and it's an effort to finish the bar, both of you silent, raising your eyebrows at each other, laughing through mouthfuls. You stand, one elbow leaning against a large, unopened box, she sits on the front stairs, one loop of her overalls undone. The two of you chew as if it is imperative to your day, and you suppose it is: you didn't have breakfast; she has more shit than you expected. This doesn't have honey in it, does it? No, you assure her, it doesn't, you checked. She reads the ingredients list anyway. That night you dream that a river of honey flows through your house, swallows you both as you sleep. Years later archaeologists display you in a museum, preserved as if in amber. Female Lovers: Death by Indulgence.

'HALOUMI': You buy knocked-down faux haloumi from the discount grocer. It looks like melted plastic, aptly so, it turns out. After the violent expulsion of your stomach contents onto the lounge-room floor you pour sawdust on the mess to quell the smell. The bag splits, and before you can stop the flow the floor is covered in sawdust. She likes it so much that after you've removed the wet mass you leave the dry wood flakes on the floor and purchase twelve more bags on same-day delivery, which she pours with a manic glee around the house. You live like this for weeks, lounging on a towel in your bikini, rubbing sunscreen on your limbs, sipping cocktails you've named Sex On A Sawdust Beach. You do not recall why you had sawdust in the first place.

LAB LAMB CHOPS: It's her birthday. The packaging unwraps and unwraps and unwraps. It's made from a thick, tar-coloured cloth. To measure it she folds in once, twice, three times around the house, continuing until the windows are blacked out and you are stuck inside. Two fists of meat, red and marbled, fall onto the doormat by the back porch. They have been grown in a lab. She passes them to you through the kitchen window, pushing aside the cloth, and instructs you to cook them on high heat, three minutes each side without washing them, letting the dirt and skin cells flaked off from your calloused feet simmer with the wine, rosemary and thyme. They will taste like us, she says. They don't; they taste like lamb. Later, when the meat has satisfied, she will use the cloth to bind your arms to the bedposts, cover your eyes, mute your mouth. You quiver at her thumb on your nipple, palm on your stomach; cry in relief at her lips on your clit.

CUCUMBER SANDWICHES: You ask her if she wants to go to the rally with you and she rolls her eyes and says what for. A beat is missed, a thin rage melts through your body. You ask what she means. What's the point? she says. For fucks sake, you say, what kind of representative are you? For vegans or lesbians do you mean? she asks while yawning. In the park where the march ends, in the shade of large cockspurs, you eat one of the cucumber sandwiches you prepared at home, offering the rest to your other friends of varying queer- and vegan-ness. Despite the cold sliminess of the cucumbers and staleness of the bread they thank you enthusiastically. Leaves fall around you at half speed, suspending time. See, you think, it's not so hard. Why don't you tell their story instead? The tree is not a metaphor.

DAHL CURRY: You make yourself dinner and at the table eat absent-mindedly while scrolling through statistics on meat versus plant-based diets, why almond milk is bad, the amount of produce required to raise animals, the carbon footprint of all the cows on earth. In a pang of injustice you think how unfair, blaming the cows. Mouth full of curry, you are bodily aware that the cuisine you are eating belongs to a country whose primary religion worships cows. Maybe you could live in India. Wait, stop. You're not a hippie, what's wrong with you? You know you can't live without your processed faux cheese and ice-cream, your First World comforts. Your phone rings. A photo of her from almost a year ago, sunglasses on head, row of perfect teeth displayed, large brown eyes—cow-like.

OREOS: The original accidental vegan. You eat Oreos standing barefoot in the yard, looking at the rainbow lorikeets luxuriating in your plum tree. From the back door: Weak. She is leaning against the doorframe. You're a weak human being she says, and then she's gone.

AMERICAN-STYLE BURGERS: As you peel each slice from its individual plastic casing, you attempt to calculate your exact complicity in the earth's destruction. What is the correct way to measure plastic used against meat not eaten (Feet to pound? Kilogram to metre? Blood let to transparency?) which is, statistically, the ethical choice? Is it better to have eaten processed, packaged, shipped alternatives or to have raised your own chickens for slaughter? What would the chicken think? After many hours with a calculator and spreadsheet, you give up.

A CRISPER OF FRESH PRODUCE: She has not got out of bed in days. You go to the supermarket, filling your basket with fresh fruit and vegetables, apologising pre-emptively in a soft voice to the cauliflower, cucumbers, apples for their inevitable demise in your crisper. When you stroll past the deli the warmth of the rotisserie chicken stand draws you in. But you don't buy one. You go to the counter and purchase the food you know you will not eat. In another timeline, you are outside, behind a dumpster, gnawing at the bones of a chicken. In yet another, the shadow of a chicken plucks in vain at feed scattered in the cages of an overcrowded barn.

THE TIP OF YOUR LOVER'S FINGER: What exactly do you mean by 'Meat Alternatives for the Motherland'? Is it because I'm British? That's very colonial of you. Am I the *meat alternative*? Are you suggesting that, because I don't have a penis, I am not meat? Am I not meat enough for you? Do you want me to have a penis? Why? So that you could eat it? Would you love me more if you could eat my penis? She grabs a paring knife from the kitchen and slices off the top of her left middle finger so it is aligned with the index and ring finger. She removes the fingernail, broils the tip in olive oil, seasons it with paprika and sumac, then cuts it into delicate slices she lays over a bed of couscous. The arrangement like the petals of a begonia. You smile agreeably and remark that it tastes as delicious as a tender lamb, the lab-grown lamb, although you can no longer recall if this is true.

A MORALLY EMPTY STOMACH: You are out with friends, non-vegan friends. The restaurant doesn't serve vegan food—not even vegetarian food. Someone asks where she is and you say, at home, she wasn't feeling up to it. You catch a conspiratorial glance from one friend to another. We haven't seen you in ages, your artist friend says. The friend whose birthday it is agrees and apologises for picking a dud restaurant, he would have picked somewhere else if he'd thought you'd turn up. Sorry, that came out wrong, he says. You've been busy, he means. You wave him off, tell him you weren't hungry anyway, your stomach gurgles, and everyone laughs. Ask yourself: at what point did it get like this? When precisely did you start making excuses for her behaviour, how you let her treat you, at the tuna hors d'oeuvres or the cucumber sandwiches? Afterwards, to get home, you pass through a park at night where a woman was murdered two years previous. You are jumpy and speed-walk. A woman approaches you, striding just as fast, flicking quick glances behind her like a bird. She hasn't noticed you yet and when your foot crunches down on a fallen branch she freezes and looks up, then laughs in relief when she sees you. You smile back, continue on your path.

HEATED-UP CURRY: Home late after walking through the park at night. You expected her to be up. You were prepared for the paranoid questions, the aggressive pacing, the loud rearranging of things that did not need to be rearranged. Instead she is asleep. You heat up leftovers to quell your moaning stomach. You realise you could, would, make this decision without her; that you care about your eating habits without her tyranny. It would be easy, you realise, the easiest thing in the world. Unbeknown to you the sun has risen and lightened the room (a new dawn has come).

A TALL GLASS OF WATER: At the kitchen sink you fill up a cup. Parched, you drink the entire thing in one long, satisfying gulp. You feel refreshed. For once, clear-headed. Ask yourself: is this an ethical story to write?

YOU WON'T BELIEVE IT'S NOT PRAWN: Holy shit I can't believe this isn't real. She uncurls the prawn from its glass, dips it in the cocktail sauce, sucks off the sauce in a faux seductive way that nevertheless does the job. At tables around you, similarly, people exclaim at the unlikelihood that No Animals Were Harmed. She laughs at your clear arousal, tells you a story about falling off the monkey bars as a kid—somehow these things are related. After dinner you hit the club—you do not remember the last time you did—dance until sunrise, walk home. She keeps you awake with a riddle. She is fun, charming, magnetic. It is easy to forget.

'COTTAGE CHEESE': You come in the door and plonk the groceries at the counter. Where the fuck were you? she asks from the couch. At a friend's, you say, and she berates you. The most animated she's been in weeks. Only her jealousy has compelled her out of bed. You turn around and leave. When you come back two days later the fake cottage cheese you bought is still on the counter, rancid. But the house plants, instead of dying, are lush and deep green. You ask her if she's been watering them and she doesn't look at you and calls you an idiot. Does it look like I've moved? Look what you've done to me. You tell her to leave. You are too exhausted to write this story.

A SWEET CHERRY TOMATO: It takes many months. Tending, clipping, watering. It's less the plants' desire to grow and more your haphazard gardening, but eventually you get the hang of it. Flowers blossom, mint explodes and almost monopolises the garden, radish sprouts happily; eventually, a small green bulb of a tomato turns orange then red. You pick it and bite into it, the fruit exploding in sweetness in your mouth. Inside the house, too, you have continued to tend the plants. They have overgrown, looping around curtain rails and cascading down the fridge, they fill the house and leave the air a clean wet mist. Ask yourself: what was real? What was dreamt? What was the moral of this story?

Orchestra of Animals

A Victorian funnel-web spider, black and round like a beetle, runs out from the metal rung on her windowsill as she slides it open. She stands there, coffee in hand, looking at its thick, latex-like legs until her cat leaps up on the counter and the funnel-web retreats into the windowsill cavity. She pulls the cat's tail through her hands as he paws at the window, and remembers the synthetic latex bodysuit in the porn she watched last week, unaroused at the steady creaking rub, thinking only about the layer of ocean floor it would twist itself into, twenty, fifteen, ten years from now—would the coral find its suffocation erotic?

I suppose you want to be fed, she says to the cat, and her tongue has a strange spasm of deja vu. This is the only sentence she has said, twice a day, morning and night, for a month.

When she worked a call centre in her youth her tongue would do this too, cramp and freeze when she'd say the same line over and over, folding itself into weird angles, not relaxing until the first sip of pinot in the evening. The tongue is a muscle, she thinks, and reaches impulsively for her phone, but it's seven in the morning, and although she knows the friend she wants to talk to will be awake she puts the phone back on the counter and gets the cat food from under the sink. From the apartment block she's watched rise for the last seven months—measuring its growth not in storeys, but the inches of afternoon sunlight it steals from her yard—the grind of construction starts up, and she wonders if she should be righteous because it's Sunday. Instead she laughs. One morning, when the building first emerged over the rusted red and brown roofs in the surrounding streets, she'd burst into the backyard naked but for her sandals and underwear. Four pigeons pecking at her lawn seed startled as she screamed, gesturing wildly, her breasts flopping every which way, *Please, for the love of god, stop blasting Kelly Clarkson. It's six-fucking-thirty in the fucking morning fucking fuck.* She'd received enthusiastic waves and the refrain of 'Never Enough' stuck in her head for the rest of the week. Then she'd thrown her toothbrush in frustration—it spun in an arc, catching in the neighbour's fig tree, sending the pigeon resettled there off into the sky. Kelly's main refrain starts up in her head again now, and she turns away from the window trying to remember where her tent is.

*

At Coles, for a twenty-litre bottle of fresh water. Plastic, she scolds herself. A few cans of beans and tuna and a bag of potatoes in case her plans to fish for her food fall through, and, after running back into the store from her car, instant coffee. She returns a third time for wine from the adjoining bottle shop. As she approaches the crossing to the car park a woman in a purple hijab comes to an abrupt stop in front of her and she pulls up so as not to hit her. The security bracket on the wheel of the woman's trolley has snapped shut, her full load of groceries halted with it. The woman looks down at the bags, then at her small child straining against her grip, yelling, crying, pleading to go back and have a ride on the escalator that descends into the underground Kmart.

She smiles at the woman, asks if she can help. The woman gives her distracted shrug. Sliding her own bag to her shoulder, she pack-mules her arms with the woman's groceries, and follows her after she's scooped up her now red-faced, crying child and abandoned the trolley in the middle of the sidewalk.

When the boot of the woman's silver Lexus shuts itself, she stands there for a second unsure what she's lingering for. Business-like, the woman asks how much she owes her.

No, no—that's not . . . She looks down at herself in her pilled flannel shirt, dirty sandals. Hears the wine bottles clinking like a wind chime in her tote bag. She tries to say have a nice day, but moves off without getting the words out right.

In her car she says a small prayer: please, ye Mini gods, get her and her car over the border without a fuss. Her car that, she knows, should belong to a recently graduated seventeen-year-old with dentists or lawyers for parents, and not to a thirty-two-year-old with a PhD. Thirty-three, shit.

She gives her Mini an encouraging pat on the dashboard and turns the key in the ignition.

*

The gods have listened, at least for now, but she's taken the long way, winding around a bush rather than through it in order to avoid any dirt tracks not reasonably crossed without some guzzling four-wheel drive; by the time she finds a suitable stretch of beach it's dark. Pulling up behind two palms, she stops on a small patch of grassy sand which separates the two trees from the vegetation behind the beach. She leans the seat back and falls immediately asleep, waking to the sun eating into her thighs. She emerges from the car to a bright clear morning. Stripping to her underwear and forgoing the sunscreen, she runs into the water in big splashes until she's waist-deep. There aren't waves, not proper ones that curl and break, only a blue horizon wobbling as if gelatinous. And the water is too fucking cold for her—even in the peak of summer, on the New South Wales southern coast. Diving in, she emerges in a shriek. Once fully submerged she finds herself happy to float on her back, thinking of the crashing Mooloolaba waves of her childhood that would tug her togs down, like the eager men she met at bars in her twenties—like she, in turn, would do to the young women she met at better bars. Waves that would take her in a tumble until she forgot which way to break the surface, gasping.

She comes out onto the beach only when her feet are pruned and soft, the flesh underneath her underwear already several shades lighter than the rest of her.

On the shore, she strips naked to sun her breasts awhile, aching with the familiar strain the swim has aroused—a constriction in her arms and chest, like a cord pulled tight. Once her tent is up, she sets about finding wood, and afterwards reads in the shade for hours, thinking she could stay right here and let the start of semester pass without her—emails from students, colleagues and heads of department filling up her inbox, at first bewildered, then outraged, then envious. The palm leaves flap up and down, big green waving hands, and she continues to read as the wind picks up and the chill erupts her skin into puckers.

She forgets about fishing for the night, eats a can of beans, cold, without looking up from her book, then two, along with half a bottle of wine, and passes out to the rhythmic croaking of frogs in the bush behind her. She dreams the ocean lifts itself into a great blue frog, white froth swirling like marble in its throat as he swells to sing to her, crashing back into the ocean and reforming in between his orchestral climaxes.

When she wakes on the second day, she has a fleeting thought of her cat being harassed and squeezed by the neighbour's kid who'd promised to feed him. She'd worried, when she got the cat, about the responsibility, a tether to a place she wasn't ready for, not foreseeing the real issue of living alone with a cat: the malevolent presence in the house. Something in the kitchen knocked over at three am. The sensation of him crawling over her half-asleep body, indistinguishable, in that state, from the original nightmare—the paralysing pressure of a demon on her chest. An ever-present feeling that her Achilles was in danger. The shock of walking to the toilet in the middle of the night and seeing a pair of eyes in the depths of her living room, illuminated in the light of a passing truck.

*

Pumping worms from a bar of soft grey sand only accessible in low tide, she sees a large flecked dog lolloping along the shore, tongue flapping out the side of his mouth. Some kind of farm dog, a blue heeler or a collie. The dog sees her and splashes into the water, a beeline toward her instead of running around the crescent path that joins to her like a natural jetty. As a greeting, the dog shakes water on her, and she laughs as he sticks his head in her bucket to lap up some of her worms, then rolls onto her feet for a pat. *Do you have a friend?* she asks, and the dog jumps up and runs around her. In the distance a man in a green shirt with a head of brilliant red hair lifts his fingers to his mouth and whistles. The dog leaps back into the water. She looks down to the sand and pumps until the black wiggling worms come to the surface, and she squats there sorting them from the grainy mud.

Fishing rod and bucket in tow, she walks north along the beach and then heads into the water, which deepens to thigh height then shallows to her ankles on a sandbar, before dropping into deep ocean. She imagines that from the shore she must appear like the messiah, half a kilometre out to sea. Now that she's found a good place to fish she remembers—to her surprise—how to cast perfectly, her finger letting go of the reel at just the right time, sending the hook and worm flying twenty, thirty metres out to sea. Her body sighing, *Ah yes, I remember this.* Now: where's Dad? But she has not been here since the monthly trips with him as a child, and he had not returned himself since she lost interest, turned towards books, friends, the possibility of art, things he had not taught her. Now all they could do was sit across the table at Christmas, talking past one another as they tried to breach an ever-widening chasm. She feels a tug and reels her line back in.

Getting the fish off the hook isn't so easy; the snapper's fin gashes her thumb before she manages to unhook and throw him in the bucket. She sucks the blood and looks down at the fish, its mouth gaping while it flops, a stark white crescent moon unable to decide between waxing and waning, arcing one way then the other.

*

Now this she feels comfortable with: the quick slice of a knife behind gills. She wonders why, for all her attempts at vegetarianism, she'd never cut out fish. How squeamish she'd become even walking past a butcher, but there was something about this, lifting the end of the cloth wrapped around her utensils, letting her descaler unroll itself out of the fabric onto her chopping board. Never managed the title of vegetarian—never been able to relinquish the taste of the sea, the flake of fish, salt of scallops, rubber of squid. A mussel sliding down her throat. And this, the methodical descale, gut, clean. She runs her hand along the plump silver white of the snapper's belly, feeling the smoothness of its scales. Picking it up by the tail she runs the spiked metal ring of the descaler, an incomplete bear trap, over the body in quick strokes—*sh-sh, sh-sh*. The scales peel out of their pockets, flecking the ground like iridescent pearls, peaking between blades of grass, spotting onto her legs.

She had stopped eating octopus at least, unable to reconcile her consumption of them with their out-of-world intellect. Those YouTube videos of octopi solving puzzles, escaping from jars, a compassionate tentacle reaching out to the big toe of its human saviour.

The childhood fishing trips had desensitised her, perhaps. Or maybe it was the bodies of the sea life, so alien and unlike her own, their gills resembling fungi more than anything.

Sliced open, the fish's silky organs burst from the seam, oozing from her hand to the bucket after she's scooped them out. The smell of fish creeps into her nose and takes residence there. She removes the head and thinks maybe—rim-shotting it onto the top of its guts—she will re-evaluate her fish-eating sentiments at some point.

A family of four emerge from the bush to the beach, the father piercing the sand with the spike of a red and white umbrella while the mother smears the two young boys in sunscreen, secures waterproof legionnaire caps to their large heads, making sure the long sleeves of their rashies are pulled down properly. The boys are their father's blond miniatures: the youngest one, with the distended belly of a toddler, even more so. The family don't seem like they are here to camp, and she wonders what has brought them so far away from the security of red and yellow flags. It is a long drive for a few hours in this pocket of the Pacific Ocean. The mother follows her boys to the water and stands ankle-deep in the shallows, clutching a large straw hat to her head and shrieking at her youngest—Bean? Dean?—for wading too far into the ocean.

She sits for a while on her camp chair, thinking of her bottle of 50+ abandoned to become warm glug in the back seat of her car. At home she applied the stuff every day, religiously, but already the skin across her nose feels taught and raw, her cheeks pink and peeling, although the rest of her has begun to brown, and last night as she fell asleep her skin was warm from the day's heat.

She watches the mother watching her sons, hand still protectively on her hat. The elder, yet to enter the water, flees whenever a wave floods the shoreline, laughing and yelling as the water splashes him. He runs back toward the ocean, and this time lets a wave pass over his feet, looking down in silence. The father removes his shirt and puts on a rashie, blue to match his sons', and she snorts, laughing, then abruptly stops. The family leaves when the sun begins to sink in an underwhelming shift from light to twilight blue. Rising to take herself to pee, she turns her back to the sea and hears a rush of water, thinking momentarily for some reason that her dream sea-frog has returned—with the voice of her mother, come to scold her for her lack of maternal instinct.

She turns around but the sea remains itself, although aggravated now the moon, plump and yellow, has come over the horizon.

Squatting behind a tree, she is almost unseated by an eerie, deafening whistle from the canopy. In a rush of adrenaline she stands up and looks up into the terrifying eyes of a powerful owl. They stare at each other awhile, she with pants around ankles, the owl in its majesty. On its face is the unmistakable human expression of disappointment, as if it has considered the weight of her soul and found her lacking. She tries to calm her heart, her pumping blood. The owl lets out another petrifying hoot, then flies away.

In the evening she lights a fire, cooks her fish, liberates hot potatoes from their aluminium shells, and watches the sky shift again into a deeper blue.

*

Soon other camps appear along her stretch of beach. An older woman, fit and sinewy, wearing an orange sarong and bikini top, perpetually holding the hand of her much younger boyfriend, both of them smiling in excess serotonin. They pass in front of her campsite a few times a day, compelled to walk in a continual pendulum along the beach the way only new lovers can. A pack of young men arrive too, four or five. A sports team? Military squadron? Maybe just old schoolfriends. They arrive three days after herself, pitch camp and immediately set about guzzling light beer, playing rowdy games of frisbee that send them splashing out to the sandbar, some unseen portable speaker heaving with top forties, and ruin her fishing spot.

After an hour with no success, she reels in her fishing line and when, walking back to her tent, she passes their site, one of them (budgie smugglers, kaleidoscopic aviators) whoops at her, swinging his hand in the air, swivelling his hips in synchronised rotation—the simple brute act of letting her know he sees her.

Mentally she's already packing up to move a few hundred metres further away from this fraternity, when another young man yells, *Braedon! What did we talk about?* He turns towards her and says sorry in a way that tells her he does not want Braedon here either. Then, *Jesus Christ, Braedon*, says a third man. Braedon starts to defend himself but she's already moved off, smiling. She'll stay put.

She sees the red-headed man around too. His camp can't be far from her. Perhaps one of the campsites further south, on the other side of the natural jetty, maybe—maybe at another camping site she knows to be an hour west into the bush. His presence on the beach is always prefaced with the keen panting of his dog. At first she sees him only at a distance. Sometimes she only sees the dog, knowing he is walking just behind in the trees, crunching somewhere along the snake of bush. It is not until nearly a week later that he passes her campsite when she happens to be there. She's lounging in the early morning shade of her tent when from nowhere the dog is there, hurtling towards her for a pat, indiscriminate paws sniffing her belongings, then bounding off to some other more urgent locale. She thinks this is another close call, but a few minutes later he passes, same green shirt, squinting in the bright sun. What she's taken for a tan at a distance is a dense layer of freckles, thickest in clusters on his nose, cheeks, the skin between his collarbones. Although she suspected this already, up close he is handsome—in an old Hollywood way, strong jaw and forehead, a not-uninteresting nose. Familiar in some way, too, and she thinks how easy it would be to invite this man over to her tent, into her life. This man and his sturdy dog. He would come over, sit beside her, and the two of them would make breakfast together, as the dog lay down panting, lifting its head to sniff at the fish on the fire. It would take only a small gesture—a flower tucked into the collar of his collie, say—and he'd be bulk buying grains for the both of them.

He waves and smiles apologetically, and she smiles back, and laughs at herself, but then looks down, folding this fantasy into the corners of her tent, because she is not capable, she knows, of properly interweaving her life with others. Neighbours that slept together, that's what her ex had said.

When she looks up again he is gone.

*

Over her last days camping she does not think about her invitation again, but on her run one afternoon she sees him bathing in the ocean, his chest reflecting the bright white sun, his hair contrasted in vivid red against the green water, and she is flooded with the thought of stripping off and joining him—anything to touch his body onto hers. At a cafe, two years from now, she will see him again, his freckles abated to a few spots, impressive sideburns, feeding a black-haired baby with red-freckled cheeks, and he will smile in recognition. She will think for a second what a nice man, acknowledging their shared accidental past camping at the same place, before she realises that she knew him—they ran cross-country together in primary school—and that it was she, two years previous, so encased in her own loneliness that she had stopped him coming over when she looked down.

On the beach, she turns away blushing, astounded at what a little pervert she's become, wanting to impose her life onto others, when she had decided, hadn't she, that she wouldn't do that. Impose with her silence and lack of people-pleasing urges. That is something her ex had given when he left: the gift of not contextualising herself to others. So now she lacked social skills that had defined her early twenties, and her friends had let her slip on this way, agreeing perhaps, some more articulately than others, she wasn't capable or willing to be more nurturing—that she was happy, mostly, in her own way.

She runs harder now, feeling the burn in her calves as the sand gives way under her feet, thinking of the things her friends knew or suspected about her. Did they know the way she could look at a one-night stand with the contempt of a decade-old relationship? Did they think she was a slut—a harlot? Someone who threw herself into sex any which way, just for the rush? A pansexual playboy, or did they just think she was confused? One old housemate had confessed that until he saw a woman slip out of her bedroom one morning he'd thought she was asexual—like a starfish, he'd said. And she'd said she wasn't sure that was true, about starfish being asexual, but was she one, though? In the sense of being able to grow back the limbs people took from her, to reject the things that were imposed on her? Maybe this way she could be a starfish. Although she certainly wasn't asexual, she had wondered about her own sexual habits. How she liked her men carved, athletic, strong-jawed; men who's blood you could mistake for testosterone, pumping through their veins. But the women she loved—loved to smell, to touch, to hold—were soft, delicate-featured, peak-lipped, doe-eyed. And these preferences had come so naturally to her; there had been no awakening, no surprise, she had not felt she needed to tell her parents, her family, her friends. They in turn never asked. It was as if they'd all known, as she had, from the beginning that this was how she was. Did she feel she occupied the space between them, the masculine men, the feminine women?

Was she anything, she wonders as she runs, aside from what she can feel? The burn in her thighs, the heaving of her chest, the tendons between bones, the muscles in her back, arms, legs. Muscles that were growing a little stronger each passing day on the beach, as she pushed her body into the sea, along the sand. What did her friends think, her family? Did they think about her at all? After three years of no serious partner, they'd stop asking about her love life, and then, as she moved, as everyone got older and coupled off, she'd let the friendships lapse, saw them once or twice a year—didn't want to bother them. Even her mother had stopped knitting in guilt trips about her lack of grandchildren.

Did they think about her at all, except for the times she occupied a seat at their kitchen table, drank too much of their wine—perhaps not. But it was becoming a little easier, wasn't it? Each time, each day, to sit with herself.

Some of the kids—young adults—in her class asked that gender-neutral pronouns be used, and they were respected and nurtured in her classroom, but she knew that support wasn't necessarily extended in the outside world. She thinks again of the family so far away from the red and yellow flags of a safe tide, and is reminded of her students. Young and opinionated with innovative piercings, wearing sneakers that look modelled on tropical fish. Despite everything, did she keep herself inside these red and yellow flags as well?

Sweat dripping down her back, she stops at the end of the sand jetty—high tide preventing her from crossing further—as she catches her breath and looks out to sea. Maybe she was the largest female groper? When the male dies, the largest female slowly morphs to fill the gender niche—no that's not right, because, as far as she was aware, a female-turned-male groper was not able to then switch back as he pleased. She was not a groper. Or a starfish. Hadn't she decided she didn't see herself in the animals of the sea? Wasn't it the muscles of the dog's back, in the skin of her cat's thigh, in the expression of the owl that she recognised something? Maybe she was wrong, and if she stayed there on the beach, she would find webbing creep up her fingers and toes, the flesh between her ribs open up to gills.

Perhaps she would find a more apt animal-metaphor had she not been coddled inside the walls of academia. It seemed absurd to her, sometimes, to be lecturing a class on avant-gardism in twentieth-century literature in a time like this. *I do not feel like I am helping,* she wanted to tell her class. *There are more important things to be doing right now.* It felt selfish to envelope herself in art—an artist could not bring insects back. Could not return land to the dispossessed, could not stop rising sea levels. What we are doing, she wanted to grab them and say: please, understand what we are doing here. Understand we are only entertainment to others—to other people like ourselves.

On the beach, the calm ocean is green and clear and blue and dark and cavernous. She breathes still more rapidly. In and in and in. Beneath her foot is a plastic wrapper—a chocolate bar. She picks it up and looks around her. There again to her left: another piece of rubbish, plastic, filth, and again, and again. *The beach is filthy!* How has she not noticed before? She runs back, stopping and snatching the rubbish from its sandy grip. She finds a plastic bag—tugs it out from its depth of sand—and fills it and fills it on her way back to her tent. And what a mess she's made! Rubbish! Everywhere! Tin cans and aluminium foil. So she cleans. Cleans and packs, as the sun sets. Filling another bag with rubbish to the light of her phone, then another as it grows darker still, and the heat evaporates from the ground. She piles everything into her car.

Folds and packs everything, leaving only the fish scales which gleam and flash in her headlights as she pulls away—and fuck, what was the date anyway?

She would leave and go back and then she could decide if she is a frog or groper or starfish or canine or if she was nothing.

As she drives, a memory surfaces from nowhere; she is not even sure it is real. She is standing with her father next to a pond. She is four, maybe five years old. He has a stone, ah, yes: the ripple-effect talk. This she remembers but, something else—he was playing a prank on her? Yes, he was playing a prank. He said, *Now what happens when the stone is thrown into the pond?* And she said, *There are ripples*—so he said, *Imagine you are the stone*, and then he gave her the stone and she threw it in—but there was nothing. No ripples, instead, a thick layer of pond scum, algae—mud, it must have been mud—absorbed the stone, accepted it without fuss, and she had stood there, horrified that the her-stone had no ripple effect.

Is she, now, a ripple-less pond, unable to affect, and be affected by, the things around her? *Oh, fuck.*

She has taken the wrong road, and swears to herself when she realises this. But it's not some pebbled red-dirt road eaten away in large chunks. Instead it's paved bitumen. As she follows it further into the trees, looking for a place to turn, she sees a balcony, and another, then the glint of someone's arm in a light—it's the straw-hat mother sipping from a wineglass on the balcony of a luxury hotel, not three kilometres from where she was camping. She stops her tiny little car filled with bags of rubbish and un-drunk bottles of wine and starts to laugh. She laughs so much she begins to cry, and worries for a second she won't be able to breathe through her hysteria. But she breathes, she breathes, and she stops laughing and sits there staring at the woman, then puts the Mini into gear and drives on. The road leads her eventually to a highway. The radio stays off for the rest of the trip home.

*

At dawn her house is quiet and dark, the morning light only just slipping in through the kitchen window. She's been gone for only two weeks but feels like a stranger in her home. Her body, returned to the lanky tan of her youth, feels foreign in her adult home, out of time. She expects the echoing of her cat's bell to greet her, but she can't find him, and when she lets herself into the backyard there are the grey feathers, but not the body, of a bird splayed across her lawn. A pigeon, she hopes, not the tawny frogmouth that visits her—although that was unfair to the pigeon. Do pigeons know, she wonders, how little we value them? Is that why they come so shamelessly for our scraps?

Now she is here again, alone, no bird, no cat, no starfish, nothing. An isolated dot under the dome of sky. She feels first the distance between herself and the next person, the next animal, is endless—then the vertigo of the distance rapidly shortening; a tradie in an orange vest pops up on top of the construction site. They stare at each other a moment, and then, together, raise their hands. Behind her, a bell jingles.

Constellation in the Left Eye

My job is simple. I place the eyeballs in the skull, I screw them into the skull, then I insert the tear ducts to hide the screws. This is very simple, although it took some getting accustomed to. That is, at first I was being too slow because, as my manager told me, I was taking it all too seriously, taking the world on my shoulders and being a *sook*. This is not a word I immediately understood, although my English is of a very good level. Far superior to that of many of my fellow workers who came here with no English at all, but I am not always good at idioms. Davina, whose job is involving the belly button, and making sure these belly buttons are to the description that the documentation dictates, she is not good at idioms either. However, she has come to understand the difference between an 'inny' and an 'outty', and is good at her job.

When I did come to understand what this word 'sook' means, I was confused. Considering my circumstances, it was, I thought, reasonable if I was being a sook. I told my manager that perhaps, if I were able to converse with my family more often, I would be less likely to be a sook, and would become, as he liked to say, More Efficient. Little Miss, he said, shut your mouth or this month you will not be able to talk to your family at all, you are currently Slowing Down The Line Of Production. I thought how he could go and insert one of the phalluses Marjorie assembles up his rectum.

This job takes a certain talent. A 'knack', as the manager calls it. It takes a knack to insert the eyes correctly so they do not appear wall- or cross-eyed. Unless, of course, the documentation stipulates that the commissioner would like them that way. Then you have to be very particular to align them at the angle that the documentation specifies.

At the time when I assemble the eyes in their sockets they do not yet have eyelashes. The head is also detached from its body, so when the belt mechanism moves it in front of me it is much like looking at a decapitated head. The eyes poke out of their sockets in horror, like the man in the video I saw as a child. In the video the man drank a glass of milk and then, looking directly at the camera, he bulged his eyes to make them look as if they were coming out of their sockets, and then a stream of milk squirted from his ducts. Sometimes when I am putting an eye in I imagine that I will squirt myself with milk. But mainly when I'm doing this I think of the man who was on the harness with me; the harness could not hold him and me and my papa, and we had been given specific instructions from the aircraft to wait calmly, there were enough harnesses for everyone. The man did not wait. Instead, after the harness had begun to lift me and my papa up, he jumped on top of me and tried to push me out of the harness so that he could take my place. The whole time, his eyes were like he had not yet been assembled eyelashes, yelling as we were lifted slowly into the air, him on top of me pushing down on my face and body until my papa hit him over the head many times and he fell, his eyes bulging. If this man had remained calm he would have had his own harness, but by the time my papa managed to get him off me we were very high up. He disappeared into the blue-black water, which then began to effervesce. I did not see him re-emerge. Yes, this is what I mainly think of.

It was difficult at first to align the eyes. But I have a good way of doing this now. First I put them in lightly. Then you have to push them very hard so you hear a slight popping noise in order to know they are properly in their socket. Then I lower my head in line with the fake head. Then I start to move the eyeballs, the left one first, then the right. I make these tiny adjustments like this, left, right, until I feel that I am staring 'into' its eyes. I know when I feel like I am looking 'into' its eyes because I will get a shudder down my spine. This is how I align them correctly.

However, when the documentation states that they are to be, for instance, wall-eyed at fourteen degrees on the left and five degrees on the right, I must use the protractor they have given me. When I am done I do not get a shudder down my spine. I merely look at them and move them on. I am often left with the sensation of incompletion.

Then there is the other factor. Their colour. I am not in charge of making the eyeballs. They are made down on the other side of the factory, in a workshop, and then put into little tubes, which suck up the balls and deliver them to me. While I am working these eyeballs whizz down the clear pipes and into the drawer under my workbench. Looking at the whizzing balls will often give me vertigo. But I will sometimes look up anyway, so I can see Grace on the opposite side of the belt. She is in charge of putting the hair on the heads—then the belt moves them around the factory, where they get eyebrows and lips and a nose, and eventually they come to me.

I am in charge of picking the right eyeballs for the job. I was reprimanded just yesterday for choosing balls too bluish in hue. Most of the documentation states clearly either brown or green or hazel or blue. But sometimes the documentation stipulates that the eyes be 'hazel-ish with a speck of blue, and an inner rim of green'; most of these specific colours are specially made. In some cases, when the head does not resemble a human but a cartoon, it will say red or purple or pink. Orange rarely comes up. I do my job to the best of my ability, picking from my drawer the correct colour. The balls are lined up in tubes of brown and green and hazel and blue, and there is a fifth tube that aligns with the fifth slot in my drawer. In this is an array of odd balls. Sometimes these are mistakes, or creative feats. Other times they are specially made. I have become quite good at picking out eyeballs that best fit the description on the documentation. Not as good as I am at aligning them, but fairly good. However, I must admit to once not putting in the right colour intentionally, even though I did not wish to jeopardise my privilege of screen-chatting with my family. While I am grateful for this privilege I am only allowed to talk to my papa, I am not allowed to talk to my maman. In my country she was a lawyer. She has proven 'problematic' in the centre and is no longer allowed to talk on the screen. But she is in good health, my papa says. Good enough. She does not weep like many of the other mothers separated from their daughters and sons and husbands. She is just happy that I can work. That I made it here to work in the first place.

I knew that by putting in the wrong eyes I was putting my privilege at risk but I could not put in the correct eyes. I could not because of the man who had come and held my face with his big clumsy meat hands.

The man had come into the department with my manager's boss, and my manager's boss's boss. It seemed that he was an important man. My manager's boss and my manager's boss's boss were laughing with their whole bodies when he said not funny jokes. He was walking down the line across the factory where the ladies cut the hair on the heads and gossip (although they are careful not to gossip around our bosses). One of the ladies, Kiera, says she likes her job very much. It reminds her of playing with dolls as a child. Even though she was a business owner previously, she is just glad she does not have to work on the other side of the factory where they assemble the groin region with fleshy flaps. There is a woman in my dorm who works down there—she used to work in the hand department but after she lost it at the manager she was moved to the department where she must arrange the flaps to resemble the preferred look as stipulated by the documentation. She is no longer allowed to contact her family. When I did not know about the incident of her ranting at the boss, I thought she was mute. Then one night she woke up yelling. Now she often hits her head on the bunk above hers. When she does this she wakes up the dorm and then other girls will throw various items at her and tell her to *shut it*, which is a phrase even those among us who spoke no English before coming here know very well. I never throw things at her.

The men in suits were walking down the line.

The important man was impressed with our work. He said, 'This is impressive.'

'Thank you, Paul,' said my manager's boss. They stopped near the knee joints and inspected the process.

I popped a mauve eye into a very young-looking head.

They walked right up near the eyelashes, on the work bench to the left of me.

The meaty man twisted a ring around his finger. 'And the eyes? They look real, move around and blink and what-have-you?'

'Incredibly convincing, I can assure you. Beyond me to explain it. You'll just have to see for yourself, won't you?'

'Haha, alright. You've twisted my leg.' All three men found this very funny.

And that is when he saw me. This Paul man. I had forgotten my work and was holding an eyeball in my hand. I looked back at my work so that my manager would not see me watching them but it was too late.

'Jenny,' my manager said, 'no privileges this week.' He turned to his boss and Paul. 'I'm so sorry about that.'

That is when he came for me. The fat Paul man. He came right up beside me and grabbed my face. His rings were cold on my cheeks. I was horrified but I did not cry. I would not let myself. I looked at him with a hate-stare. And that is when he said it.

'Such beautiful eyes.'

He did not let me go and I clenched my jaw. I could feel water gathering in my eyes. Then before I could cry he took his hands away.

He walked back to the two other men. But I did not hear what he said. My ears were fuzzy and I was taking large breaths. And they were whispering. Then in a minute my manager came over to me and I thought for sure this would be it. I would never see my papa's face again. 'Good work,' he said. And the three men walked off.

Half a week later something horrible happened. This is when I intentionally did the wrong job, and I am now worried.

I was doing my work. Inserting the right-colour eyes. Aligning them. Putting in the tear ducts, moving the heads on down the belt. I looked up to the screen. The documentation stipulated that I should put in hazel-green eyes. 'Speckled,' it said. With a specific dot of yellow on the right eye. You might think me stupid to not realise straightaway what I was doing, and I admit I did for a second feel a wave of familiarity cross over me as I read that, a 'twirl in my stomach', so to speak. But I did not think too deeply about it as it was four o'clock in the afternoon and I had been at my job for hours. I began looking in my drawer for the correct eyeballs. I knew I could find the left eye quite easily in the hazel compartment, but the right one would have to have been specially made. Sure enough, after I'd found an appropriate left eye—it was speckled with brown dots, like the night sky is with stars—the right eye rolled down the fifth compartment. I plucked it out. Then the head jolted to a stop in front of me. It wobbled a little bit but did not fall over, they never do.

Even then, I did not really recognise the loose curls on its head, or the curve of its nose. I placed the eyeballs and then popped them in with my thumbs. Then I lowered my head and began to align them. First left then right then left again. In little increments I worked and then I removed my thumbs and stared into the eyes and shuddered. But this shudder did not stop at my spine. It went through my body, my spleen, my Adam's apple, my knuckles, my fingers. Nothing was left unshuddered.

I sat in horror looking at my own head. Looking into my own eyes. My double's mouth gaping. Ready for its intended function. Like that, we must have been quite the sight, for I too had my mouth gaping. In shock. And my eyes must have been staring out also, like I too had not yet been assembled eyelashes. For a moment I was frozen, unable to yell out. But then I stopped being frozen and I did what had to be done. I unpopped the eyes. This was difficult. The eyeballs are designed so that they cannot be accidentally dislodged while the doll is in use. I had to pivot the eyes out with a screwdriver. This took me a while, and when I was done each eye had a deep scrape perpendicular to the iris. I knew I was holding up production. I knew that my manager would be down soon to see what was holding up production.

When I got the eyes out I looked around frantically for different eyes. Eyes that would not make this doll me. I found some grey ones. They were blank, lifeless. I popped and aligned as quickly as I could. I heard my manager's footsteps down the factory line.

'What's going on?'

I put the tear ducts in and moved the head along. The next head was coming and the documentation above me changed. He would not see what I had done. His footsteps were almost upon me when I looked down and saw my own eyes, scratched and rolling on my workbench in front of me. I grabbed a third eye, a dark brown one, and leant over. I stuffed the two damaged eyes into my socks. It looked as if I had oddly bony ankles.

'Jenny, what are you doing down there?'

I straightened myself up. 'I am very sorry, sir. I lost an eye and had to look around a while to find it.' I presented the brown eyeball on my palm.

He paused and looked down at the eye. He bent down and peered under the bench. I did not cross my ankles. 'Alright then,' he said, and left.

I prayed he would not glance at the head to my right in front of the eyelash station. My prayer was answered: there was a commotion at the toenail line and he was gone.

I keep my eyes in my socks. Every night I take them out and hold them. Stare into them as they stare into me. My right eye with its yellow dot looks just like my real one, but my left eye is different. On my left eye, the scratch from the screwdriver goes all the way to the iris, cracking the surface and splintering the eye colour with countless hairline fractures that meet in little white dots, like stars. I used to think the irises of the eyeballs were made of glass, but the way this one has shattered underneath the surface, like there is a constellation right there in my left eye, I am not so sure.

A Dog's World

If she thinks about it, a dog only ever knows what it sees of the world, so the dog's world *is* what it's seen. Maybe, she reasons, dogs can smell the rest of the world? When they smell a bird, or the residue of a bird, they know the smell came from something they have not smelt before; so then they smell the outside world into existence. Or maybe, she thinks, it was just that dogs keep up with current events, *haha*. Snoozer did like to watch the news with her—he was just the cutest, smartest dog, her little baby. Maybe she herself has been underestimating dogs as a species. So a dog's world isn't just what it's seen and experienced; it doesn't just cease existing, stop being programmed, like those video games her son plays where the character can't go past certain doors or walls or clouds because things beyond that point stop being. Well, that's what she used to think about a dog's world. Not that she'd really thought about it before, but if she had she probably would have thought that. Snoozer just didn't have the outside world programmed. But now she thinks maybe dogs have rich inner lives just like humans, or, in some circumstances, richer than humans. For example, is her world only the Woolworths she works at, and the fifteen-minute stretch of road between there and her flat? And everything else just doesn't exist? Because, if she really considers it, she hasn't stepped off that same path—out of that existence—for at least three months, and only then to go see her mother or to her son's school when he misses the bus. Or rather, when he missed the bus, before he got himself into trouble. And, she supposes, the vet last night. Maybe right now her world is even narrower than that?

On the couch she sits on every night watching telly, with the blinds closed to stop the glare from the streetlights outside, she wonders if that outside view, closed off, is no longer part of her world—if it shuts down when unseen, like a computer in power-saving mode. Maybe, she thinks, if she went over and opened those blinds quickly enough she would not see the street and her neighbour's cat perched on the window but just, nothing. Not even black space—although, she supposes, nothing probably is all black. Or all white? No, she decides, black. And when she does this—walks to the blind to open it and peer out— she thinks how she hasn't been inside her son's room in a very long time and, so, does that part of the house still exist? Is it a part of her world if she ceases going in there?

She looks out into the dead grass, the brick letterbox, the wilting wattle. She can't see the cat in the neighbour's window opposite. The cat, of course, is somewhere else, because other places *do* exist. Of course they do, she knows this, and she knows if she walks to her son's room, which she is doing now—or hobbling, really, pain shooting up her knee—and opens the door she will see the grey carpet, the god-awful poster, the computer set-up with her son on his reclining chair saying, You could knock, what do you want? And she will smell his room, maybe even before she opens it, which is really bad, really very pungent, the smell, no matter how many times she's asked him to air it out. If she does open the door they will get into a fight. Maybe because his bed sheet is disgusting, or because he will in that very second have some unsavoury photographs on the computer, or videos, even though she's told him not to do that. She's told him it's wrong, it isn't real. Or maybe he will start calling her a fat piece of shit, as he has taken to doing recently, which is rich, them being the same size, and him a lot lazier. Couldn't he see that it is for him that she works the job that's given her knee pain and not much money and not enough time to cook? Those things were all for him. She does try to save up, but the cremation has emptied her bank account. When he moves, she thinks, she will drop a shift, have time to cook and clean. She will get back in shape, get her figure back, that wonderful figure she had, until he came along and distorted it. Then the tables would turn, then they would see who was the fat piece of shit, *haha*. Not that she would ever say anything like that to her son, never—although he's said a lot worse to her. But, she knows, he never really means it.

Outside his room she doesn't need to open the door to be reassured he is in there, existing, because she can hear shooting and her son cussing at his friends. Instead of being happy that he is not loudly watching porn, which he has stopped even pretending he doesn't watch, instead of banging on the door and telling him to please keep it down and watch his language—haven't they talked about how he talks about women—she is just relived that her son and his room still exist.

And so, instead of opening her son's door and getting into a yelling match, instead of going back to the couch, she goes to the kitchen. She thinks about the places she hasn't seen in there in a while. It is getting to dinnertime too. He will be hungry soon, and she doesn't want a repeat of the evening before when she fell asleep on the couch after coming back from the vet. (She will have to go tomorrow again, but she does not want to think about that, not right now.) Last night she woke up to the front door slamming, him calling her a bitch and saying he took money out of her wallet to go get KFC, because, he said, she couldn't even make fucking dinner. She had disconnected the internet after that. When he noticed he called her a slut, screamed it at her really, opening the door of his room just to slam it, then started blasting that horrible music. The disrespect in her own house—unbelievable. He had never spoken to his dad like that. She'd yelled at him through the door and told him to get a fucking job and get out of her house or at least go back to school and there had been no reply except the throbbing of that music. She continued yelling, knowing she should stop, that she shouldn't have started in the first place.

In the kitchen, before she sees if all of the places in the cupboards and nooks still exist, she pulls the pizza out of the freezer and then out of the cardboard box and unwraps the plastic bit that's always a pain in the arse. He hadn't really meant it, not really. And she couldn't blame him for the fact that he had never learnt how to put a frozen pizza in the oven. How had she not shown the boy in his whole sixteen years how to do that? God, how was he even going to look after himself? She will show him later. So she puts the pizza in the oven and goes around to check if all the nooks and crannies exist. And they do, or otherwise she cannot catch them out. She even fakes going to open one cupboard and then pulls open another, but there are still cups and plates in it and not a black abyss of nothing.

He hadn't taken that much from her wallet last night, only enough to buy a meal and he had even left her some chips. A half-hour or so after the yelling match she was watching *I'm a Celebrity*, thinking how she had watched that entire thing, the whole series, without even giving a shit—television was the only way she knew how to unwind. The show ended and she turned it off. Feeling guilty, she got up and turned the internet back on. After ten minutes or so she heard him calling from his room that he'd bought her chips and they were in the fridge. Maybe, she thinks now, looking at the pizza through the oven door, if she asks him nicely, he will do some chores around the house this week. He could do some more chores around the house in general if he isn't going to school. Maybe he can start thinking about TAFE next year. She won't bother him with that right now, though, she will give him a little break. He is her son, after all.

While waiting for the pizza to cook she walks back to the living room with thoughts of returning to the comfort of her couch. She almost forgets about the lack of existence of everything outside her world, but then catches sight of the side door she never goes through, because it opens to the staircase. Her left knee does not like the staircase, and even though they live on the second level of the building, she can walk out the front door and go over the footbridge that joins up with the street in front, then loop back around to the driveway. The slope isn't great for her knees but it isn't like the stairs—nothing is as bad as the stairs. She turns now to the side door, looking back at the oven. When was the last time she went up the stairs? Not once since Tom left. Her frozen pizzas were always undercooked when she pulled them out, so maybe if she gives this one a few extra minutes it will be hot in the middle, and then he wouldn't complain—for once, *haha*. And maybe they could even have dinner together—she smiles, that would be nice. She starts up the stairs and immediately a sharp pain shoots up from her knee to her hip. It's as bad as when she has to bend down at work to get more bags from underneath the counter. Sometimes when the pain is really bad she makes a wounded-animal-like noise, like *uuuuug*. The sound repulses her, reminds her of the noise her mother makes when she's digesting, beating her chest after a meal, but she can't really help making the noise—it just started happening when she bent over one day. But right now she thinks her knee can just go ahead and deal with it, even if it means weeks of hobbling around and making it worse by having to stand on it at work, so up the stairs she goes. Maybe she will ask for a chair to sit on at the checkout. It's against store policy, but she's been there thirteen years and she's never asked for anything. Except, she supposes, to go home early when he gets—got—into shit, but it's not like they didn't know she had a kid, or about Tom, and they were pretty understanding, and did they expect her to just let her boy wait at school with no way home? No, she would never do that. Not that she had to anymore, *haha*.

Pulling up on the fifth floor with one floor to go she allofasudden feels bad because she shouldn't *haha,* he had to finish school. Surely. Maybe if she kept telling the school he was sick for now, he could go back next term? Just one or two months off. Which wouldn't be great for his grades but was better than nothing. She is almost at the roof now, bending over to reach the makeshift doorstopper; straining, she emits the *uuuuug* noise and loses her balance, her knee clicking out of place. She clutches at the doorframe for steadiness, leaning all her weight on the door handle, and nearly falls through the doorway to the ground. But she finds it—steadiness—and then, after using her foot to secure the doorstopper under the door, walks out onto the roof.

Feeling the air on her cheeks, flushing from the cold, she is overcome—almost to tears—when she sees the city lights speckled out in front of her like through the door of her microwave when he forgets to take the alfoil off the leftovers. Oh the beautiful night! And the mountains she can see over there in the distance, on the horizon, only just discernible against the darkening sky, the spindles of trees on the mountain smudging its outline. All these things existing outside of her! The noise of cars sounding overworked, with overworked people inside them. The bird's nest against the drain, no bird present, but a distant chirping. She sees and hears and smells all this and thinks of course the world is bigger, *of course* it is because she can go wherever she wants if she wants to and it doesn't shut off. It is always there, waiting. She thinks maybe she will go to that mountain there and see it, look at those trees and see the city existing from another perspective, from that angle over there. While thinking this an airplane goes overhead and she looks up. She stands there thinking,

thinking about her son and her poor dog and about the people up there in the plane—thinking maybe someone is looking down from their window and seeing the speck of her on the roof, and just maybe that they are wondering about her, about her life, about the places she exists in.

Intermission I:
All the Stories I Started but Never Finished Because of the Time-Restrictive and Distracting Nature of the Gig Economy

A woman rings her mother. They talk for a short amount of time before the woman hangs up. She does not call her mother again for four months.

A beautiful short woman has a child who grows up to be taller and far more beautiful than her. She is in turn elated, worried, and conflicted about the waning of her own youthful beauty. All this happens before the child turns five.

A woman has her friends over for a large feast. She has many friends, all with various food requirements and allergies. Nobody dies or unknowingly eats animal products.

A woman's life is controlled by her phone. This is not unusual.

After being raped in her own bed, a woman drags her mattress around with her as protest.

After being raped in her own bed, a woman drags her mattress around with her as a protest. Realising this has famously already been done, she begins to drag around all the mattresses women have been raped on. Within seconds she has too many mattresses to carry. She piles them up in a stack and climbs atop them to protest. While up there, she falls asleep. Someone places a pea between two of the lower mattresses. Metaphors are mixed.

Rather than following her dreams, a woman pursues a job with financial security. Many years later, she is still unsure if she made the right decision.

Rather than marry a poor man she loves, a woman decides to pursue a relationship with a man who can offer her financial security. Many years later, she realises she made the wrong decision.

Rather than marry a rich man she has no feelings for, a woman marries the man she loves. Many years later, she realises she made the wrong decision.

A woman only wears black.

When a woman who wore bright colours in her youth marries, she begins to wear only black. Nobody asks her why.

When her husband dies, a woman who wore black throughout her marriage begins to wear colours: dresses of deep plum, jewels like pomegranate seeds, greens as varied as the forest. When someone asks her why, she says she was mourning her own independence.

A woman tends to her garden.

An unidentifiable fruit grows in a woman's garden.

A woman has to explain the exact nature of her sexuality and gender politics to a large group of strangers. This is her worse nightmare.

What is worse, patriarchal or capitalist structures? Can they really be separated? One woman reports.

A lifelong vegan has the insatiable urge to eat human flesh. Chaos ensues. She is also a woman.

A lifelong vegan has the insatiable urge to eat human flesh. She eats her boyfriend.

A woman tries to figure out what the men-to-women ratio is in vegans. In the end she discovers gender is a construct.

A person figures out they prefer not to be gendered. This is all very confusing because they've been writing a short-story collection about the intricacies of being a woman, or a certain type of woman, or maybe not being anything at all but instead the ramifications of womanhood in a complex system of patriarchal and capitalist oppression that makes women like them, or people like them, both a victim of and culpable in violence against other women, minorities, animals and the earth. They wonder if it wouldn't've been more feminist of them to just write two hundred and forty-two pages about how bad sex offenders and billionaires are.

A couple go on a road trip.

Two sisters go on a road trip.

Two cousins that may as well be sisters go on a road trip.

Two friends who may as well be sisters go on a road trip.

Two friends who may as well be sisters go on a road trip. It is revealed they are fleeing an environmental disaster.

Four months later, a woman calls her mother back. She tries her best to explain why her feelings were hurt without raising her voice.

A woman meets her ex-husband's new wife at a baby shower. They become good friends.

A woman meets her ex-husband's new wife at a baby shower. They run away together.

A woman cleans her cupboard.

A woman remembers to clean her kids' lunchboxes before summer break.

After summer break, a woman is unable to identify the contents of her kids' lunchboxes.

A woman wants to have children but, considering the climate crisis, decides against it.

An empowered woman doesn't want children; the world is on fire.

An empowered woman doesn't want children; the oceans are rising.

A woman has never wanted children but still feels a deep sense of loss; she mourns her inability to want children; she feels not empowered, but hollowed, in her lack of maternal instincts. The natural world is collapsing at an alarming rate.

Two women fall in love. History is not ready for them.

Two women fall in love. This happens at a point in history where they are free to express this love openly, and only bigots are angry about it. The natural world is collapsing at an alarming rate.

A woman having marital issues reads a book about a woman who leaves her husband. She leaves her husband.

A woman having marital issues reads a book about a woman who leaves her husband. She decides, while reading it, to leave her husband, and then, as she ends it, decides to stay with him.

A woman reads a book and realises she is the main character. Chaos ensues.

A woman reads a book and realises she is a side character. Hijinks ensue.

A woman repeats herself. Nobody listens.

At the beginning of a relationship, and then multiple times throughout, a woman states explicitly what she wants for herself, and what she expects from her partner, long-term. Many years later her husband says, 'I don't know what you want from me.'

A woman buys a large bird. They watch the telly together and during the ad breaks remark on the weather.

A young woman buys a large bird. After many decades of companionship, the woman becomes a notorious revolutionary and climate activist. At the end of her life, she relates her memoirs to the bird. The bird, struck with grief, is unable to relate these stories to a biographer, and her history is lost.

A young woman buys a large bird. After many decades of companionship, the woman becomes a notorious revolutionary and climate activist. At the end of her life, she relates her memoirs to the bird. The bird, not having the ability to mimic human speech, is tormented with his inability to tell her story to a frustrated biographer.

A notoriously messy woman cleans her room. With each layer of debris, she uncovers mementos and reminisces.

A notoriously messy woman cleans her room. With each layer of debris, she uncovers mementos and reminisces. The memories are revealed to be false.

A woman decides to be an artist, but because of the climate crisis is not sure this is the right career path.

A woman decides to be a writer, but because of the climate crisis is not sure this is the right career path.

A woman decides to be a social worker, working with troubled youths. This proves to be the right decision, but because of the climate crisis she grieves for the lost futures of the teenagers she works with.

A woman decides to be, but because of the climate crisis is not sure this is right.

A woman decides to be a corporate lawyer. If she notices the climate crisis, she doesn't say anything.

A woman is born. She doesn't know it yet, but she will be the last human to live out the length of her natural life. She becomes a dentist.

A woman decides to be a scientist. Thank God.

A woman can't orgasm. The natural world is collapsing at an alarming rate.

All the women you know get together to play a game. Sitting in a circle each woman, in a clockwise direction, relates a painful memory of unwanted sexual attention, harassment or abuse. The game stops when the next woman in the circle has no more memories to relate. This game goes on for many months.

Oh well, a woman thinks to herself, I'm sure he won't do it again.

A woman's life is controlled by her phone. Chaos ensues.

A woman falls in love with her phone.

A man falls in love with a woman. She is a cyborg. Things do not go well. Alex Garland's lawyers get in touch.

A woman has a son. As a young man he commits an atrocious crime against a young woman. Everyone blames the woman.

A woman has a son. As a young man he commits an atrocious crime against a young woman. The son does not blame himself.

A woman has a son. As a young man he commits an atrocious crime against a young woman. The rape victim's mother blames the woman.

A woman has a son. As a young man he commits an atrocious crime against a young woman. The woman blames herself.

A woman lives her life guilt-free. Discuss.

A woman can't decide if she respects another woman she sees every day. Eventually, she realises she's been looking in a mirror.

An old woman delivers an apple to a young woman. The young woman lets it rot in her fruit bowl.

An old woman delivers an apple to a young woman. It is from the old woman's garden. This is an act of kindness.

A woman steals an apple from her neighbour's tree. Her neighbour was intending to give it to her anyway. No harm, no foul.

A middle-aged woman disguised as an old woman delivers an apple to a young woman. Chaos ensues.

A middle-aged woman disguised as an old woman delivers an apple to a young woman. Chaos ensues in that Disney sues me.

A woman sets out into the rugged wilderness of the bush to find meaning. Chaos ensues.

He does it again.

A girl can't decide if she wants to grow up to be a virgin or a whore. The men in her life call a conference.

A woman falls in love with a deeply troubled man she insists has a good heart. Although he gives her many reasons to leave him, she never does.

A woman falls in love with a deeply troubled man she insists has a good heart. Although he gives her many reasons to leave him, even at the insistence of all her loved ones—her sister, her brother, her mother, her childhood friends, her local greengrocer—she never does. 'He loves me,' she says as the bruise on her nose yellows, de-mapping itself from her eye sockets.

A woman falls in love with a deeply troubled man. Many years later she realises he does not love her back. She has no practical skill set or support system. When she explains this to a police officer, he drops her home with a wink to the husband.

A woman falls in love with a deeply troubled man. Over many years he erodes her support system, independence and self-esteem. He wins the custody battle.

A woman falls in love with a violent, petty, narcissistic man. At the trial his lawyers call him 'deeply troubled'.

A woman falls in love with a violent, petty, narcissistic man. After many years of physical abuse, gaslighting and controlling behaviour, she still insists he has a good heart. In a faraway village, another woman dedicates her life to reassembling the shattered remains of porcelain dolls.

A woman of fair complexion asks women of darker complexions to help her.

A woman of fair complexion asks women of darker complexions to help her. She insists she must join the men of fair complexion, who, she knows, are on a higher platform, up there—she points upward—just out of sight. Under her instruction, the darker women contort their bodies into a staircase, mutilating their arms and legs until they fit the desired configuration. When the staircase is at last big enough, and the darkest bodies at the bottom of the stairs are cold and hardened, she trots up the staircase and leaps the final step onto the higher platform. 'Don't worry,' she calls back, 'I'm leading the way.'

A Tight Schedule

Something annoying: my teenage daughter has developed anorexia. There is no time in my schedule for this. Every morning, Yoseph emails me my schedule and nowhere in there does it say 'talk to your teenage daughter about her eating habits in a healthy and conducive way'. Yoseph is new; there is no way for him to know this. But Allie—she would have put it in there. She knew my daughter. She would, twice a week, come to my house and check on my family. She would, when I had an event, make my teenage daughter and my almost-teenage son dinner while I was at such an event. Their father is no help—if I had it my way I would have forgotten his name. I would only remember him as 'the man who almost never washed his bed sheets', or better, 'the man who *always* finished first'. Some people are under the impression that because my children are three years apart and look very similar, and do in fact have the same father, I have an ex-husband or ex-partner of sorts. This is incorrect. I had a brief affair with an artist (he is attractive—better, he makes very attractive work) and fell pregnant. I was pregnant once before but chose to terminate it. This made sense: I was young and my career still depended on a few opportunities to become a stable reality. However, when I became pregnant with Madeline my life and career and finances were stable enough for me to have a child and still work. I was the editor of a high-end lifestyle magazine. I had private health care. I went to the dentist just because. The current editor of that magazine was my protégé. I am very proud of her. As for me, I have, as they say, moved up in the world, to an international magazine. I am editor-in-chief; I have a place on the board, I hold stocks. I have worked in the industry for over twenty-five years, at many magazines, journals and newspapers in a variety of roles. I have a very busy schedule. After Madeline was born I continued to have relationships with men who were not her father. However, when Madeline was two I met her father again; the arts section of the magazine did a profile on him. I informed him he was the father of my child; we had another affair and I became pregnant again. I realised that this was a unique way for Madeline to have a one-hundred-percent blood-related sibling. Having a second child worked well for a few years. As with Madeline, I took maternity leave until Louis was old enough to be looked after by a carer, Susan. God bless her soul. Susan is no longer with us, she was deported. When I returned to work I resumed my old position, and continued to work in an industry I love. The second time around I informed the artist that he was the father of my child. I told him he should in no way take this as an indication that I was 'in love' with him. At no point should he misconstrue the fact of my having two children with him as indicative of my being in some way infatuated with him, or with his work. His work was impressive, sure, but frankly not my thing. He took this well. I sometimes maintain a sexual relationship with him. He occasionally does not finish first. When he is in town he sees the children. The children are aware he is their biological father but they do not call him Dad, they call him Marian. He is more of a friendly donor or family friend than their father; they do not rely on him for typically 'fatherly' things. They do not need to. I can do it. That being said, my teenage child and my almost-teenage child more and more do not call me Mum. They call me Veronica, or sometimes—I suspect ironically—they call me Mother. My children are very well off. They live in a four-bedroom apartment on the seventeenth floor of a very nice building. The building is nicely furnished. The couches are antiques. The paintings could be in museums. At first the children were a lot to handle—I knew this would be the case. I was prepared to put in the extra effort, and step back from my career if necessary, in order to take care of them. Some people may not have noticed this; however, I know male peers who have not been prepared to do the same thing. For instance, my male colleagues can stay back until seven, eight or even nine at night to finish a project. They can 'pull an all-nighter' if they have to. I cannot do this. I have children who need to be fed. I am beginning to think Yoseph will not cut it. We will see. So far my schedule is not progressing the way I was hoping. The role of the PA is to adapt. To realise my own needs before I do. Thus far he has not accomplished this. They are good sched-ules—yes, sure. But they are not *great*. They are by no means *ground-breaking*. They do not at any point include 'meditate for fifteen minutes' or 'remind your teenage daughter to pack herself lunch', or even 'help her pack lunch the night before school, and then *remember to check if she ate that day*'. Sure, they have plenty of '7 am meeting with J. Laron @ Cafe Prestige', but no 'sit down and check in with your daughter about her relationship with the other girls in her class'; 'Ask her if she feels comfortable at school'; 'Ask your daughter if she would prefer to go to a specialised high school or college of sorts'. There is none of this. As a result, I do not have the time to ask her such questions. Perhaps she wants to go to an arts school. I know she wants to be an actor. Although, I am unsure if this wanting to be an actor thing is a state that every vain teenager goes through (and they are all vain) or if she is genuinely *entiché* with dramaturgy. Does she have favourite actors? Does she know the amount of dedication and time that goes into the craft of being someone you're not? *Convincingly?* Or does she just like the idea of having a harbour-side apartment with a pool? And if acting is just a whim, or vanity, is she interested in anything else? Does she have a hobby? Would she like to go to a different, non-all-girls school? I have always had doubts about all-girls private schools—my son goes to the 'brother' school of my daughter's. I suspect these schools are not doing what they purport, which is 'preparing students for an ambitious, passionate future in the profession they *want* to pursue', but rather 'turning them into entitled little brats who think everyone owes them everything and that they will just be *given* whatever job they want because they call the education minister Uncle Toddy and not A Wanker'. I myself went to a public school and did just fine. Boys were never a distraction—or not a big one. I knew better than that. However, I suspect my teenage daughter does not know better than that. I suspect this is because she is only exposed to boys other than her little brother through school dances and the internet. And more often than not she is grounded when these school dances are held. As a consequence, she has become far, *far* too aware of how she appears to them, these mythical 'boys'. As a consequence, she does not seem to be putting effort into her *mind*. She is yet to be enlightened as to the depth of knowledge one is capable of holding in one's brain. I thought about this when I enrolled her. I looked for elite co-ed private schools. There are none. Why is that? People who don't hang around people of the gender they are attracted to can become strange. It would be handy if she was a lesbian. Or if she at least shared a schoolyard with boys—if she had some kind of exposure. Although even with her brother I am noticing there is not too much exposure. They do not really connect or bond in the way I imagined siblings would. I have no siblings, so I cannot tell. That being said, I have a friend who was my childhood neighbour. Her parents would often volunteer to look after us, and vice versa, when the need arose, and I think we would have spent 24/7/365 with each other if we'd had the chance, but we did, after all, live in different houses. Trina is like a sister to me. She was often the one who—when Allie was not available—would come over and look after my children, although she can't do this all the time, she has children of her own. She lives just around the corner, actually. But her children go to the public school. I am thinking of sending Louis there. He does not get along with his sister and he does not get along with his class-mates. He is very withdrawn. He has a very big heart, though—I love him very much. I know I'm not meant to play favourites.

But I am struggling at present. For instance, while I was prepared to put in the extra effort as a mother when the children were younger, looking after, as you have to, their wellbeing and checking up on them and grooming them into respectable adults, I did not realise I would still have to be doing this when the children were older. When they are on the verge of becoming adults. I thought, for instance, that once Madeline was smack-bang in the middle of puberty I would not have to hire a babysitter. That she could—hypothetically—*look after* her younger brother. This is not the case. Instead, if I have to go away for the weekend, I send them over to Trina. But when something resembling an emergency comes up at work, I leave them alone. But only after talking to Louis. This is our deal: Madeline *thinks* she is in charge, and no doubt bosses him around the entire time, telling him to do the dishes and not telling me about the plethora of friends she has over, which she does *all* the time—although I don't think she's game enough to have a boy over. Yet. She wouldn't know what to do with herself. Yes, she is ostensibly 'in charge' but Louis is the one who makes sure they have dinner on time, and enforces—or at least tries to enforce—my no-internet-after-nine-thirty pm rule. Personally, I don't like this rule. I don't like telling my teenage daughter that she should not be texting boys she *hasn't even met* about stuff she doesn't know *anything* (Heaven Please) about. God help her if I ever catch her sending nudes. No, I do not like this rule; I would personally prefer to be able to trust my teenage daughter with a little self-control. I would like to think that she could put her phone down and not send eggplant emojis well into the am. But as it is, I cannot trust her. Also: who decided eggplants resemble penises? Historically, they've always been closer anatomically to a zucchini. And the eggplant resembling an *egg?* Who made this emoji? Have they ever seen an eggplant? Or a penis? I would like to know. Maybe I will have a word to Yoseph about this—the schedule, I mean. After all, he is new and he cannot know all these things. Sure, Allie did not have to be told that in my schedule thirty-five minutes should be allocated for exercise, and another forty-five for bonding time with my children. She did not have to be told that I could not go to such-and-such because I had a parent-teacher night, and parent-teacher nights are not optional. Not if you care about your children. She did not have to be told that I couldn't attend the launch of the new architecture magazine because I was busy being told by the school counsellor just how my parenting was making my daughter *act out.* Allie did not have to be told that I was not capable of enjoying champagne with my colleagues because I was being informed by the school chaplain—the idea of whom having *any* alone time with my children was frankly alarming— that my daughter's rapid weight loss might have something to do with all the pictures of insect-thin women I have strewn over my living room. What, so I shouldn't advertise my accomplishments? Shouldn't be proud that my *entire life* has been dedicated to something I'm actually good at? And I told this chaplain just as much too. I also informed him bluntly that just because I send my children to an Anglican school does not mean I, or my children, are even *remotely* religious, and I guaranteed him that in the future my daughter would not attend 'mandatory' religion classes, and just try and expel them, see what happens. They are great students. Madeline at least doesn't fail—she gets solid B-minuses, which are far from expulsion grades. And Louis, well

Louis is an A-plus exemplar of a student—a student who will no doubt go on to be an A-plus exemplar of a human adult, who will no doubt be someone the school, in the future, will want to hold up on a pedestal as having been one of *theirs*. However, I am beginning to think that they will not be able to do this much longer. That I will send him to the public school down the road. It's a good school, despite what the other parents say. There are fantastic teachers, and the students, the good students, really want to *make* something of their lives. They are not just sitting around waiting to be given shit like they deserve it. I will have a word to Yoseph about this. I am not being fair, after all, we can't all be Allie. I will tell him about my issue with my daughter. I am thinking maybe I will tell him I *have* a daughter. He may not know. He might think I am a bad mother for this. But the fact is, the men in my department have children—Gerald has *six*—and you wouldn't know it unless you specifically enquired: *Do you have children? What are their names?* The reason Yoseph does not know I'm a mother is because I am aware of this unwritten rule, and I am also aware that if I go endlessly on and on about how much I love them it will be seen as a *weakness* instead of a strength. Yes, I will ask Yoseph to schedule us a meeting, and I will, instead of firing him, explain my situation. I will tell him that I have two children. I will tell him that I want to send Louis to another school where he can relate to the other children. I will tell him about my fear of Louis becoming one of those sunlight-deprived men who live with their mother until she kicks them out at thirty-seven. The type who go on to complain endlessly about women's body hair on the internet. Although I will also tell him that I know, realistically, this will never happen to Louis. That my son is smart, and has agency, and is too much of a little feminist himself to become this type of man, but I will tell Yoseph about my insecurities nonetheless. And I will tell him about *her*. She. Madeline. I will tell him about my daughter's anorexia, I will tell him about her stealing that poor girl's phone and sending unsavoury photographs she found on it to everyone in her grade, and to a high percentage of the grade below. I will tell him about the little spots she has all over her face all the time from throwing up whenever something goes even vaguely near her stomach. I will tell him how my own mother had anorexia, and would, when I was growing up, constantly make comments about the portion on my plate, how it looked like I would have to go up a size, and how that size was approaching a size ten, and that would be a problem if I ever wanted a decent man. And I will tell him about my own anorexia, and how I overcame it. And how, recalling what my mother said to me, what she did to me, I *never* said *anything* about my daughter's body. I made it my business to make my daughter body *nobody's* business. But that somehow, because the universe wants to punish me, she has developed anorexia nonetheless, and is in rather urgent need of attention. I will tell Yoseph to schedule her an appointment with a shrink, or a GP. I will get him to look up what I am meant to do here. I will get him to schedule a nutritionist, the country's best nutritionist if that's what needs to happen. I will make sure Yoseph allows time in my schedule *every day* to check in with my daughter, to see how the girls at school are treating her, how she is treating the girls at school, to check if she is okay, and we will get to the bottom of this. I'm determined we will fix this. We will fix this.

All Noise Through the Fog Will be Forgiven

Here she is again, then, Vivian, crowded around a bar table. Looking down, she's been careless, decorated the tabletop in moon cycles. She looks over at Lucy, sees one single rim of condensation in front of her, watches her friend flick her eyes down to place her cocktail in the same spot. Mindful, no doubt, of the waiter tasked with clean up. This makes Vivian smile: of course, something like this is second nature to Lucy. Good Lucy, who catches her smiling, grins also, but then turns back to her conversation with Patrick. Vivian watches sunlight catch on Lucy's head, transforming her friend's otherwise brunette hair burgundy, and this makes her smile more.

She tunes back into the conversation she was, hypothetically, in the middle of and sees the end of an eyeroll from Brianna to Christina, the meaning of which is clear to her. The conversation moves on before she can call Brianna out on it, and she knows, now, she never will. This has happened more and more recently. She needs to be on her guard. She shouldn't have to be, among some of her oldest friends, but she does. She knows how her friend has begun to think of her. Vivian is prone to these things—becoming distracted or withdrawing into daydreams— but Brianna, she knows, believes this behaviour performative, and treats her in a way she feels that warrants. God knows to what end this performance is supposedly intended. But, but, Vivian can't invest herself in the cruel things her friend is thinking. Too many characters, too many anxieties, too much of a fog, when she needs to leave space for work tomorrow. And she can't get too drunk; she's already on her third—fourth—and needs to switch to water soon.

'So, pretty much moved two floors up, in charge of half the people I used to work with, which is, y'know, fine,' Brianna wraps up. 'A little weird.'

'Congrats.'

'Cheers.'

Vivian uses this to re-enter with more gusto, raising her glass in celebration, which summons a small guilty smile from Brianna—a truce, perhaps. There she is, Brianna, suddenly twelve again, already in Vivian's kitchen before she's home from school, eating the Vegemite and tomato sandwich Vivian's mother has made before driving the two of them to acting class. Same smile: whoops, love you, forgive me.

Brianna works at a bank and her promotion is why the five of them have gathered on the opulent banks of the harbour; this configuration is not the norm. Christina and Lucy are not particularly close, and despite their industry contacts, Christina and Vivian openly hate each other. Patrick, Brianna's boyfriend, often becomes overwhelmed by these drinks with her girlfriends, each of them getting steadily drunk as if it were a task to tick off, cackling, clapping, yelling over the top of one another. Tonight he's game, though, keeping pace with beers in tall, frosted glasses.

Still, they are all Brianna's inner circle and there's cause to celebrate, so Vivian, despite her building resentment, has turned up.

'Oh, does that mean you're in charge of that bitch who narked on you?'

'Yup.'

Christina opens her mouth wide but does not actually gasp— she does actually waggle her eyebrows, which makes Vivian give a cruel puff of a nose-laugh. Christina does not acknowledge this. It's no secret, really, why some of Brianna's nastier personality traits have been overriding her more forgiving ones lately; Vivian sometimes feels the urge, like a parent, to call Christina a bad influence. It is ironic, perhaps, that Brianna's parents used to say the same thing about her. 'Lucy,' she has found herself wanting to say, forehead collapsed to a maternal frown, 'she's a nice girl, why don't you spend more time with her?'

When they'd all sat down upon arriving at the bar, Brianna had not chosen the chair Lucy had obviously left free for her, but the one on the other side of Christina. The kind smile Lucy gave Patrick as he sat down beside her devastated Vivian. Made her remember every time the two of them, Brianna and her, had become loud, uncouth, shrinking down Lucy's presence.

There's a trio of women—girls, maybe, they look young, although these days anyone under twenty-five looks like a teenager to Vivian—sitting at the table over. Wasn't it scientifically true that twenty-four-year-olds still have the same brain elasticity, same room for development, as teenagers? She's read that somewhere, she's sure. That the group of girls recognise Christina is obvious, all of them carefully not looking at her, periodically having fits of giggles. The waiter, in his erratic glances, recognises her too, although is maybe having trouble placing her. In fairness, it is hard to place someone who is known for doing nothing. Christina's influencing briefly landed her a recurring role on a long-running soap opera. Vivian had made Lucy watch an episode of it with her, just one, to confirm what she already knew: talentless. No spark. Her climatic scene: Christina's character, driving on the highway, pulls over dramatically when her boyfriend forgets something—a present for her mother? Her favourite food?—something inane. They get into an argument on the side of the highway. It was hilarious. Her ridiculous pout, her voice licking up at the end of sentences, bitingly Australian in the way no city dwellers spoke anymore. Even Lucy had let out a shriek of laughter when Christina's big moment, crying on-screen, culminated in squeaking her lines through fake sobs, dry eyes in her hands. Lucy, of course, was immediately overcome with guilt, covering her own face in penance as if to mirror the scene before her. Even by the standards of the show, Christina was not good, and her character soon died in a freak jetski accident. She had, Vivian thinks, gone back to being professionally narcissistic.

Christina is doing that now, tending to her hundreds of thousands of followers. She takes shots of herself and Brianna pouting, clinking glasses, pouting, clinking glasses.

The girls at the next table are posing in the background. One of them, Vivian is sure, will soon crack, lean over and ask for a selfie.

Alongside them: the gentle murmur of waves, which coalesce when a ferry goes past into a loud hum. The rippling wake hits the pillar of concrete just below where they sit and sprays upward, cooling them in salty mist; they have prime seats at the edge of the restaurant, overlooking the water. The summer sun is still high enough in the evening to justify the strappy tops they are all wearing. Except Patrick, who's wearing the uniform of young urban professionals, although he is not one. On his collar there's a damp patch where he's dabbed away beer.

This is a shock to Vivian, used to seeing him in khaki shorts and T-shirts whose logos have long since faded. In Patrick, Brianna's best self is reflected. It's clear he's made the effort to dress up. Of his own volition, Vivian hopes. That Brianna chose such an affable kind-hearted man speaks of her compassion, however buried it has appeared of late; that she is constantly fighting an internal battle with self-interest is hard to overlook.

Brianna, talking with Christina, lets out a large, beautiful laugh, and Vivian wants then to lean in, rub her hand on her friend's knee. But she stops herself. She is not ready for anything that implies forgiveness, not yet. Brianna and Christina are becoming more enclosed, her friend is turned ever so slightly away from her. Over the course of the night, Vivian predicts, she will lean more and more into Christina, until her back is to Vivian. The pair of them are deep in conversation. Or Brianna is, at least; Christina never has much to say. If she does, it is generally gossipy, cruel comments about other people's appearance, their skills or lack thereof. Although not even Christina can bring herself to be mean to Lucy, nobody can. Lucy, pretty and smart but not, God bless her, threatening. Christina tried it on with Vivian exactly once, shortly after she appeared in the group three years ago. Brianna had brought her along without asking to celebratory drinks, not unlike this evening: Vivian had just got the leading role in a short film, an independent that would do the festival rounds here and overseas. Which is to say, a short film that was well written and not made by rich kids with Tarantino fetishes. Off the back of it Vivian had been offered an audition in LA, and had quit her waitressing job the morning she learned she'd landed the role.

'Wow, that's impressive. Did you have to wear makeup to your audition?' Christina had asked her, sipping her drink with a cool, tight smile. 'I wish,' Christina said, in the brief second in which Vivian was too shocked to reply, 'I had the guts to go makeup-free all the time the way you do.'

'It's a shame,' Vivian replied, 'that you don't have the personality to stick to your own nose.'

Ever since then, Christina and Vivian speak to each other only in too-polite small talk; the atmosphere between like a vacuum, in which only that previous interaction exists.

Brianna scrapes her chair back and says, 'Have to pee.' Lucy, attuned to even the slightest drop in social atmosphere, turns and folds Vivian and Christina into her conversation with Patrick.

'Patrick,' Lucy says, 'has figured out his population drop.'

'The frogs?' Vivian asks.

'The frogs,' he nods.

Patrick's an ecologist. He works in urban green spaces, monitoring biodiversity and protecting animal populations. Green tree frogs are his personal favourite, and his and Brianna's place is full of small models—glass, ceramic, stone—of frogs. Walking into their apartment was for Vivian not unlike walking into the home of an eccentric grandmother. The contrast between Patrick, with his short-back-and-sides and reserved manner, and his home décor, never fails to amuse Vivian.

'So. What about the frogs?' A grin. She can't help it.

Patrick shuffles in his seat. 'Well, okay, at first we were convinced it was the new highway causing the rapid decline. Frogs trying to cross—*splat*. So we've spent *months* making plans and getting approval for tunnels—drains really—from the park to the wetland on the other side of the highway, even though these frogs don't generally travel a lot. Stay in the same spot most of the time. So the tunnels are ready, the frogs can cross, great, but the population continues to decline. Then we think—predator? Kids, maybe. There's a new estate nearby. Maybe the kids are getting bored and coming over with Dad's golf club. Something like that.'

'Jesus,' Vivian says.

'Yeah, horrible, right? But it's not that. The kids *are* coming over and sure, they're loitering and being pests, but they're not doing anything serious. Like they're not interacting with nature, is what I'm trying to say. They're just sitting around on their phones, bored. Maybe looking for shrooms in the wet season. But mainly they're just smoking weed, talking shit.'

'So, they *are* interacting with nature, then?' Vivian winks at Lucy, who immediately bursts into laughter.

'Ha, sure. Aren't we all?'

'So, it's not the kids?'

'This is when we realise we're looking at the data all wrong. Some of the frogs are being picked off by natural predators, but the problem isn't so much that they're dying, it's that they're not being born in the first place, because they're not mating.'

'Your frogs aren't horny?'

'My frogs are—libidinally challenged, yes.'

Lucy's face goes red from suppressing giggles, her dimples appearing to radiate. She doesn't normally drink so much.

'Something in the water?'

'We did think about that. Like pollution preventing egg fertilisation.'

'What are we talking about?' Brianna, pulling up her seat.

'Frog sex life. So that's an easy fix then. Put on some jazz, pour some tiny glasses of red wine.' As she says this, Vivian raises her own wine as if to salute the frogs, smiling at Patrick.

Brianna looks at Vivian with pure malice. The shock of it turns her silent.

'That's just natural selection though, isn't it?' says Christina, bored, checking her phone. 'Like, boohoo, sorry frogs. That's life.'

Lucy looks anguished, Patrick inscrutable. He lifts his glass, takes a sip and says, 'I'm not sure it's that simple, really.' He's at ease with life, unbothered by the indifference of others.

The waiter comes over; they all lean back and move their glasses aside to make room for a plate brimming with oysters. For Lucy there's a small bowl of olives.

Christina and Brianna both declare the oysters look delicious, flirting with the waiter as if in a game, because they could not, ever, be reasonably expected to flirt with waitstaff.

Phones are unholstered; the conversation moves on.

'Another round then?' Patrick says.

'Stay put, it's my round.' Vivian pushes herself away from the table. As she's leaving, one of the young women at the next table says a bold, 'Excuse me.'

*

Snorting coke off Brianna's house key, Vivian did not, she reflects, successfully transition to water. She's crammed into a toilet cubicle with Brianna, Christina and Patrick (Lucy did not want to participate, but thank you) in the back of whatever night-club they're in. Patrick looks unperturbed at being herded against his will into the women's bathroom. Upon Brianna's request, Vivian forked over the contact and five hundred dollars, shudder-ing while withdrawing the cash from an ATM: an old habit from being an out-of-work actor. In reality, she would never, truly, be out on her arse—her parents have money, she has money. She will not check her bank account tomorrow, and by the time she does will barely miss the dent.

Spilling back out into the club, they go to the bar and purchase lavish, fluorescent cocktails that each of them, in turn, forgets in some dim corner of the room or presses into Lucy's hand, claiming they can't drink a thing. The coke is good. Lucy is plas-tered enough that the difference in their highs is unimportant; they can all dance, easy. And they do as much, before the coke mellows and they take another line, two; the coke turns out to be the chatty kind. They get sick of yelling over one another on the dance floor and abscond to the smokers' area where they bum cigarettes off strangers as if it is a matter of national impor-tance. Lucy and Brianna sing along to the song leaking from the dance floor, a nostalgic pop punk hit from their teenage years. Vivian asks a stranger for a lighter and is subsequently pulled into a debate about the gender of Pengu, the titular penguin of the long-running children's TV series *Pengu*. Christina is just standing there, swiping through her phone, sucking on a cigarette, swaying. Patrick disappears, and twenty minutes later reappears brandishing his own pack of cigarettes, as he does whenever he's inebriated, although he claims to have quit years ago. Lucy, her eyelids on two separate frequencies, asks Vivian, 'Donchuhavewommow?'

'What?'

Lucy sucks in a big breath. Shakes her head. 'Don't you have work tomorrow?'

'Shit.' It's two am.

Brianna looks at her. 'Do you have a shoot tomorrow, Viv?' She seems, incredibly, hurt.

'Yeah. It's nothing. I'm barely in the scene.' This is untrue. 'I—I actually have to go. I'm sorry.'

'Okay. Goodnight. Love you.' Like she means it.

'Love you too. I'm going to take Lucy home on the way, she's—'

'Tanked.'

'Yes.'

'I'll help,' Patrick says, frowning down at Lucy, who's now standing, eyes completely shut.

They leave through the smokers' exit. Vivian flips out her phone and concentrates long enough to order an Uber. 'There. Four minutes.'

'Okay. You alright, Luce?'

Lucy nods but does not open her eyes or say anything.

'So, you got another film? That's great.'

It is great, but the question is there: Why didn't she tell Brianna? The truth is, she doesn't tell Brianna much at all to do with her career anymore. It doesn't always inspire the best response. She has not told Brianna she came back to Australia just to work with this director. Brianna assumed that things weren't panning out in LA, and Vivian did not correct her. She hasn't told her about the shoot because she doesn't want to upset her, ruin her celebration of a promotion in a job they all know she hates. A job that she had got, after a few years of a comms degree she never finished, in her father's bank, having not thought much about what she wanted to do with her life—if you didn't count the acting classes they took together as kids, and neither of them do. Vivian has found that when she does tell Brianna things—what she's auditioning for, how much she's being paid—Brianna replies, 'Wow, that's all, really?' Or she tells Vivian she can't expect to get the part if Mia Wasikowska is also going for it, sorry. It's the type of response that is hard to take issue with when it's so much a part of Australian culture—making sure your friends don't grow too tall.

'Yeah—listen. What about the frogs?'

'The frogs?'

'Did you figure out what the matter was? Why they weren't mating.'

'Oh yes! Right. Noise pollution.'

'Noise pollution?'

'From the highway. They couldn't hear each other croaking. Or their songs were interrupted.'

'Their croaking wasn't very erotic.'

'Exactly. You weren't too far off.'

'What?'

'With the frog jazz.'

'Really?'

'Well, no. But we did have to play them frog noises.'

'That's hilarious.'

'It's fine now, though.'

'Fine?'

'Well, no, what is? They just croak louder. It's deafening. There was an adjustment period, I guess.'

'Right. Ah, we have to go, Lucy are you ready? Uber's here.'

Patrick helps Lucy into the back seat. Vivian slides in next to her, and he gives them both a perfunctory wave before turning on his heels.

'Hi,' Vivian says to the driver, 'we're making two stops.'

'No problem.' The driver is the silent kind who does not ask how their night is going. This suits her fine.

'You alright, Luce?'

'Yeah, I'm just going to close my eyes, though.'

'Okay.' Vivian opens her phone, goes to Instagram, presses on the little red circle above Brianna's name. She watches herself replayed from a few hours ago. It's a strange sort of ritual, Instagram stories. A form of time travel: in this version of her, her hair is still up, as is the sun behind her, she clinks glasses, posing, pouting from two, three, four different angles, flattering and not. She experiences the out-of-body feeling, the vertigo, of watching a video you were not aware you were in.

Christina, unsurprisingly, has no qualms tagging Vivian in her story. She has not, however, tagged Lucy. Lucy with her modest feed of her dogs and vegan meals and three hundred followers. Vivian looks through her own archive of videos and photos and posts the best from her night, picking flattering ones of Brianna. This is their love language. Vivian thinks of the way her friend had looked at her in the bar, with so much hatred—or did she imagine it? It had been a problem during their teen years, the amount of male attention Vivian received. Although to her, Brianna is the more obviously beautiful one. At the time she'd handled her animosity by growing body hair, never wearing makeup, things she'd kept up in her day-to-day life between shoots. Although she'd stopped wearing baggy pants, grown her hair long, and no longer quoted Judith Butler at the slightest provocation. How much more could she cast off for her friend? Discard her accomplishments? If she slashed her own face and got a mindless desk-jockey job, would Brianna love her again, then?

The Uber pulls up outside Lucy's house.

'Do you want me to come in with you?'

'No. I'm fine. Love you. Goodnight.' Lucy is upright, eyes wide. She kisses Vivian on the cheek, says, 'Text me when you're home,' and leaves.

'Can you just stay here a second?' Vivian says to the driver and sits there, the car idling, watching Lucy let herself into her house, closing the door behind her.

*

'Miss. Miss. Please wake up. You have to get out of the car. Please.'

Vivian sits up, awake. One of her nipples has ridden up, cresting above her top.

'Oh my god.' She reaches for her bag, leaps out of the car, which is parked outside her apartment. How much time has passed? 'I'm so sorry. Sorry.'

The Uber driver looks relieved, he puts his hand up to cover the sight of her nipple. She tucks her breast back in. If you could call them that. Mosquito bites. 'Sorry,' she says again.

'That's fine, fine. You get to bed now.'

Vivian turns, fumbles for her keys, walks down the path along the side of her building. How did she fall asleep? She checks her phone. Three am.

A hand grabs her shoulder; she screams.

It's the Uber driver; his hands fly up to the don't-shoot position.

'Sorry! I didn't mean to scare you. I called out, but you didn't hear me.'

'Oh.' Vivian's heart races. 'You scared me.'

'Yes I know.' The driver's eyes glaze over. He lowers one of his hands to give her something—her wallet.

'Oh,' she says again. And before she can say thank you he's already left.

She lets herself in to her apartment, strips off her skirt, throws it on the couch, and pours a large glass of water.

In three days, Brianna will text her, a random assortment of emojis asking how work went. The hangover and comedown Vivian will sport the next day for her scene, one in which she plays a bereaved and battered woman, will earn her a best-actress nomination in no fewer than three film festivals, two of which she will win. She will tip the Uber driver thirty bucks. She will forget to text Lucy. All will be forgiven.

She walks into the lounge where she sees herself, a ghost reflected in the dark window. Her blond hair falls to her elbows. She feels just how she looks: transparent, weightless. Below, behind her reflection, the traffic goes on, back and forth like a tide. This close to the beach, the sounds of the ocean and the main road mingle together, are impossible to pull apart. Through the nonstop murmur of the city, what isn't she hearing? Is she missing something?

Women I Know

—My god, darling—the women I know. *So* sensitive, let me tell you. As if their hearts will burst the second I suggest they're being a bit, well . . . It's not like I think all women are hysterical, don't get me wrong, darling. I've been around the block; I've been around the block a few times. These men, that's what they want us to believe. To think. Can you pass the ashtray? Don't ever start smoking. My god, not with your skin. That perfect skin. Has your mother let you audition for anything yet? No? Oh, don't listen to her. You'll be famous before you're twenty with a beauty spot like that. Never even light up. Never even start, that's the trick. I'll tell you why. Here's what they don't want you to know: smoking is wonderful. No, really, it's wonderful. Beautiful. It's the only thing holding me together at the moment. It's the only thing I look forward to at the end of the day. With everything going on. Which is—what I'm saying about these women, what you have to understand

101

about these women, darling—they just don't get how it works. They just really can't stand how it works. They could do with a cigarette and a tall glass of gin, if you ask me. Instead of leaping into flames the moment something—Anyway. Oh, don't listen to what they're saying about your father.

—I know, Grandma, it's okay.

—God, if people talked about them that way they'd call it a witch hunt. It's like they expect politicians to be, to be, well, I don't know, *inhuman*. Completely without fault. Higher than thou. And the way they talked about you, love, the way they talked about *you*. It's just completely uncalled for. I mean, whatever happened, *whatever happened* to *dignity* in this country? No, I think it's a good idea that you stay here for a little while. Completely unfair, like any of them could stand having their life examined in that way. I'd like to see them have *their* perineum examined by the public. That's what it's like, darling, basically.

—I know, Grandma, it's okay, really. Is that a birdbath? In the backyard, behind that tree over there.

—Of course you're so well adjusted, look at you. You could do anything you set your mind to, and *still* your mother hasn't let you audition for anything. Not surprised, if I'm honest. But don't worry, love, she'll come round.

—Back there by the garden next to the what-you-call-it. Those bushes. Bougainvillea.

—Although these days they let anyone be a model, don't they? Talk about standards. Hardly have to go out and try with Instagram and all that rubbish. I mean, really, all you have to do is pose semi-naked, and done, you're a model. Not like you, not like the natural beauty you are. Darling, I'll talk to your mother about it. I'd talk to your father about it but he's got enough on his plate at the moment. What with half the country leaping to castrate him.

—. . .

—Not that anyone has ever considered *his* feelings. But don't worry, I'll talk them round. I'll talk your mother round. They've got good sense. Good sense. Don't pay attention to those newspapers. Now, would you pass the ashtray? It's getting rather urgent. That crystal one there, by the window. Next to your elbow. Darling, what is it you've done to your hair?

—Is it a sundial or a birdbath, there beside the bougainvillea and tomatoes? No wait, tomatoes don't grow on trees.

—Persimmons, darling. Gifted to your grandfather on behalf of the Greek community when he served as local representative. Not that they're even Greek, originate in China apparently. Lord knows, honestly. A nice gift nonetheless. Back when he was on the local council, nobody gave a tosh about your private life. They fall off and collect in a big rot at the base of the tree. The smell is *unimaginable*. Don't know how many times I've asked Jeffery to do something about it. *No ma'am, there are too many of them.* Oh Christ, please.

—Can we make something with them?

—If you wish, my love, we can make persimmon pie to your heart's content if that's what you want.

—I'd like that.

—Are you sure you're okay, love? You don't quite seem yourself.

—. . .

—Oh no. Oh no, please don't be like that, love. Everything is going to be alright, really. It will all pass in the end. What you have to understand, darling—well, maybe you shouldn't *have* to understand, but what you have to understand about these people, these women I know, they don't know anything about civility. About *manners*. Trust me. Strutting around in—well, you could hardly call them clothes. And don't even get me started on their personal hygiene, or body hair. Speaking of, love, what *have* you done with your hair? Lopped it all off— with a hacksaw by the looks of it. And after we'd finally bred some decent hair into the family, so thick. I remember when I first met your mother I was a little, well, you know how she can be, love, but I do remember thinking, What *hair*. What hair. Long and thick, golden yellow, healthy all the way to the tips. You're very lucky. Could have ended up with my wispy thin nonsense. The amount of hairspray I've gone through in my life. Look at your father, practically bald now, although with all the things coming at him it's not a wonder. I was looking at a picture of him from last year, and it's alarming really, how quickly he lost it. But it's not something that men have to think about. No, he couldn't even imagine how much money I have to spend just to look presentable. Not that anyone looks at me anymore, at my age. Here.

—. . .

—Oh god, my leg is cramping, let me adjust. Oh my god, don't take those young legs for granted, dear, go for a walk. Go for a walk out in the bush, I don't remember the last time I could— it's really quite pretty out there. Oh yes, yes that's better. Bloodflow. Now, what was I saying? Oh yes, it's not surprising really that these women are so up in arms about everything. I would be too if all the men in my generation were addicted to pornography. Disgusting. How do you go with the boys at school? Not that you should be wondering about boys at your age. Not just yet, no. Although, I suppose you can't help it. Just ignore that question. Ignore me. Well, here's some advice: don't start looking at boys before you know how to drink properly. Just trust me on that one. Although actually you shouldn't be thinking about that. Really, *what* have you done to your hair, darling? You know these days cutting it that short . . . Well, people will make *assumptions*. That's all. People will make assumptions. You haven't cut it because—well, are you okay, love? Is there anything you want to talk about? I know this must be hard on you, I do. That's why I think it's good you've come to live with me a while. It's nice to have you here, love. Besides, I could do with the company. It's the best thing for the time being, so we don't have another incident, hmm? So we keep our hair on our head, yes? Just until this all blows over. I know this isn't a fun time for you, but it will pass, eventually. I know it doesn't seem like it right now, but it will. God, the way people talked about you. As if it's ever okay to talk about an underage girl in that way. And some of the comments, darling. Some of the comments online. Jeffery showed me on his phone. I couldn't bear it. That they'd talk about you in that way. Animals.

—. . .

—Well, don't listen to them anyhow, darling. We can have some fun together. Jeffery is also teaching me to cook these strange Spanish dishes. Delicious. And don't worry about your mum and dad. That's—it's not your job to worry about them, it's their job to worry about you. But. I know they're spending some time apart, but I think maybe that's for the best. Don't worry, your mother will come around. I know everybody's primed to file for divorce these days. Let me tell you, some of these women, ready to go off at the *soonest* available—honestly, it's ridiculous. Mind you, I'm not saying divorce is a bad thing, no. Back when I was young if some of the women could have . . . The way their husbands treated them, *handled* them. Well, it wasn't that they couldn't have, darling. It's more that people would talk. Oh, I remember Lily divorced her husband, barely saw her again. She had a few dinner parties with us, would come to visit us for a while. But then she stopped. Moved, I think. I was one of the lucky ones. Wouldn't have divorced your grandfather even if I could. Life can be a bit dull now without him, love, let me tell you. Actually, now I remember, Lily moved to Melbourne and—ha! You know, my darling, I think she became one of these women I'm talking about, the ones that started popping up in the sixties, those hippies. Started to go to all those gatherings. Someone said that someone they knew saw her and she'd lopped all her hair off! There you go, my love—you've got something in common with Lily. Ah, see, I knew I could get a smile out of you. I remember we all didn't know what to do, none of us did. You'd see some of the other women, they'd leave their husbands. Stay with their sister or something. Claim they were going to divorce him—but. They always came back. And I think for a while we all thought that was what was happening with Lily. Just a stage. And that Lily would come back.

Because how was she going to support her children without Liam? Anyway, we all waited and waited, but, well, she never did come back. Liam eventually remarried. As far as I know, she could still be down there in Melbourne, with her ridiculous boots, carrying on like that. Ha! You know, she could be one of these women who so desperately want your father to resign. Carrying on. Although your grandfather always liked her. Me and her, well, you have to understand, honey, that in those days friendship between women wasn't really—it was odd. A little too competitive, maybe. I never really felt connected to a lot of those women. That's not necessarily the case anymore, is it? Your mother said you've got quite the group of friends, quite the group of girlfriends. They aren't terrible to you, are they? Teenagers can be. They aren't, are they? No?

—...

—That's good, dear. That's good. Although I suppose you're sad you won't be able to see them. Is that it? My dear, don't worry, you'll see them again, don't worry. Please cheer up. It's just, it's a good idea you stay here for a little while. We can pick some persimmons together. We can pick them together and make something. You can find a recipe on the internet. Is that nodding? Can I take that as a yes? Okay, I'm taking the nodding as a yes. You know, with these women. Some of the things they're saying. It's all very. Some of it is like, Good god, pull yourself together, this isn't—everyone makes mistakes, is all. I know some mistakes are worse than others, but, well. Sometimes people aren't happy. They aren't happy the way I was happy with your grandfather. And sometimes in a marriage, when people are older and things aren't good, they look outside—they look for something else. Even—even those of us who are happy do that sometimes. It's not something to be proud of. But, and I know it seems like what your father has done is *evil*, I know you're not very happy with him at the moment, darling, that you don't like him very much at the moment. But he isn't evil. It's just, at some point you have to ask, How much is any of this anyone's business, really? I don't think it's fair, having to announce your marital problems to the world. Although, some of the things these women are saying about him . . . I know you don't like your father very much at the moment, I'm not sure I do either. This isn't the way I raised him. Some of the things they're saying he did, I don't believe it. I don't want to believe it. It's not the way he was raised. You know, I have never been glad about anything the way I am glad your grandfather is not around to see this. He would be *very* upset. Very disappointed. If what they say is true, darling, he would be disgusted. Not that I should be talking to you about any of this. I just—some of his behaviour. The way people are saying he acted. It's not the way he was raised. But, well. When I was a secretary—did I ever tell you I was a secretary, back before I met your grandfather? Well, I was a secretary at this hoity-toity law firm. And the way some of the men there behaved. *Well.* It isn't a surprise, really, a lot of this stuff that's come out. This isn't new behaviour, darling. Not new behaviour at all. Although you'd like to think it was just a few small instances. It's just I don't believe your father could—your grandfather did not raise him that way. I think maybe sometimes, I think, Was it me? Did I cause it? Your grandfather used to say I spoiled him. And maybe I did.

I couldn't have any other children. Having him was a miracle in itself. A miracle. Maybe it *was* me. But that doesn't mean I taught him to act like that. I didn't teach him to do those things. You know, sometimes—sometimes I think if the men were acting like they did in those days, and with things the way they are now . . . I wish your grandfather was still around. Sometimes I think all the good men are dead. Now, would you please pass the ashtray, my love, before I have to butt out in my gin. Look, I've got ash all over the place, what a mess.

The Shape of _____

When she was nineteen, a man her father trusted approached her in the frozen-food aisle of the grocer. He walked over while placing spinach in his basket. Instead of acknowledging her with a curt nod, he stopped and smiled. He told her he'd been feeling lonely since his wife left him. If it was alright with her, he would like to have her over for dinner. He would cook her authentic ratatouille, a dish he had learnt during his tenure in France. He would pay her, in cash, four hundred dollars to do so.

That night she told her father about the man's proposition. She did not mention the pay. He said that he was a nice man. She should go and listen to him complain, he was just lonely.

The next evening, she put on a silver dress, silver shoes, a silver hairclip, and a large white coat with faux-fur lining. On her arrival, she pressed the doorbell. The man opened the door, looked her up and down, and chuckled. Come in, he said. He was wearing the pants and sweater of a retired businessman.

He led her through to the dining area on the second floor. They sat on an enclosed balcony with floor-to-ceiling windows that overlooked the dense forest of the mountains. From there you could see down a valley to the tops of trees covered in snow, hear the eerie roar of wind tunnelling through the trees, branches batting against the glass. The snow made her feel more ridiculous, as if she'd intended to look like a winter nymph, just wandered out of the forest. He sensed her self-consciousness, and said she looked lovely, to not be embarrassed, he was sorry. He appreciated her taking his request seriously.

Within five minutes of starting dinner, he excused himself to the bathroom. When the man came back, his penis and a thumb of his shirt tail was hanging out of his zipper. She could tell from personal experience his penis was neither small nor large, it was an exceptionally average penis. Circumcised, the colour of a faded bruise, hanging just so to the left, a vein running down the centre and breaking off into small branches, like a river drying up. She did not say anything about the penis and soon understood she had done the right thing. Throughout dinner, he talked of his son and daughter. He was a personal trainer, she studied nursing, they both looked like their mother, although Claudia had got his nose, poor bugger. His ex-wife got only partial custody but now the kids had left home they only ever called for money. He couldn't blame them, really.

When dinner was finished, his knife and fork resting in polite parallel in the middle of his plate, he thanked her for coming, cleared the table, wished her a safe drive home and waved goodbye from the driveway, his penis still hanging out like a forlorn slug. She slalomed her tiny car down the mountain roads, her headlights hitting the bright white of the fresh fallen snow that flashed in reflection, like a million animals staring out at her from the dark. The animals, of course, were not there, but in hibernation, or on the lower parts of the mountains where snow did not fall—and as it did, for just one week of the year, mid-winter. Once home, she passed out for ten hours, still cocooned in silver.

A few days later, she got a call from the man thanking her for coming. He did not ask her over again but said he had a friend who could use her services. If she would like, he could pass on her number. She said nothing, and then said okay, sure. He thanked her again and hung up.

Like this, she soon lost control of the momentum of her life. People—men—put her in a certain position, and she made no effort to change the course of this decision. Her job was not quite sex work, although it was often of a sexual nature. At first, it resembled that initial job. She would go over to an empty house and be invited to do laundry, or watch the news, naked. Heavy breathing might emanate from a nearby locked door or it might not. She would organise a kitchen cupboard, scrub a bath, or clean an entire house in her underwear. Over time her work changed. Sometimes she would just keep a man company, listen to his problems, no dangling penis, no need to take her clothes off or moisturise her body in front of a man salivating—his wife out of town. Mostly, she listened. The men cried, but also did not. Sometimes she let them massage her feet or tuck stray strands of hair behind her ear, but mainly she sat or walked with them as they told her how their marriages had broken down because of their infidelity or poor communications skills, because of their poor communication skills and infidelity, because their wives were crazy bitches who robbed them of the best years of their life. Because they had fallen out of love in such small increments they could not remember what it was like: the beginning of infatuation, the butterflies, how they'd felt on their wedding day—the idea that they would be with this woman forever—the way that had disintegrated day by day until the most exciting thing that happened was their wife making spicy hummus or suggesting they watch the latest James Bond. Maybe the wives left them for richer, older men, but more so, younger, poorer ones. Other times the men had never been married or loved, and this was the primary source of their despair.

She was not, nor had she ever claimed to be, a therapist. She suspected that was part of the appeal. Rather, she imagined herself sitting somewhere in the middle of therapy and sex work, although she was qualified for neither. The pay was certainly as decent as a therapist's or sex worker's, so she would say—when pushed to clarify—which would you prefer?

Since the beginning, she relied on word of mouth and was never short of work. The mountains were populated by people with too much money, or not enough, but who were desperate enough to give away what they did have. They had bought and built up mansions, or had nowhere else to go, seeking refuge from the law or their own shame. In these hilly, dense lands, there was the other part of the population too: families that had lived there for generations, and young nature enthusiasts who had settled here to have children; the latter would sell weed to the boomer population of hippies still dazed at the accumulation of their own wealth. There was also a small but distinct community of Christians, bordering on a cult. They kept to themselves. Although she belonged to the population generationally attached to the landscape, had grown up twenty minutes away from where she now lived, her life revolved around the former populace: those that came with money, or criminal records, in common, a chronic loneliness.

Soon, almost a decade had passed, and her life was not something she recognised. She had let other people mould her. A liquid filling slowly into the shape of a woman she had not seen before. That season, the wetness of La Niña made the autumn colder. Mist hung around in fog all day, and, when the rain fell, it fell on the burnt timber forest of the fire season just past, two extremes, eroding the landscape unrecognisable, the sounds that emanated from the mountains changed too, as bird populations pushed to the edges of town rebuilt. Monday mornings, she was paid to learn origami from a man who was either a former drug dealer, violent criminal, or both; he was evasive on the matter. His mother, he told her, had taught him origami, one of his small comforts as a little boy. But he had found, since he came here, it did not soothe him as it had as an only child, distracting him from his isolation, but made him acutely aware of his own solitude. He lived in a caravan out of town and paid her weekly in cash, after asking her to step outside while he retrieved it from its hiding spot.

Monday evenings she cleaned a house for an old man while listening to him talk about his dead wife, his estranged children, the war he'd come back from a murderer. He did this while watching TV, sitting in a worn chair two feet away from a flat-screen so large it was clear he'd taken up the habit decades before, when television sets resembled boxes and required constant twiddling. He would fall asleep mid-sentence, periodically waking up and resuming exactly where he left off, before he fell asleep one last time around nine o'clock. She would finish scrubbing his dishes, turn the television off, take the envelope of money from the kitchen drawer on her way out, and walk home along a long road, the gentle splashing of a creek bed humming behind the trees.

On Tuesdays and Thursdays, she helped a convicted paedophile garden. The paedophile—Terrance—was particularly fond of roses. He favoured yellow and pink for their fragrance, but enjoyed having every colour in his lush, isolated garden. That he had family money was obvious. His house was the only one on a long, narrow road, the driveway branching off for another kilometre at the cul-de-sac. His remoteness meant that he need not worry about the community petitions to have him removed; there were no scowling neighbours rushing their kids past his gate, spitting in his direction. No bags of dog shit left or set on fire at his front door. His primary concern was the soil acidity of his labyrinthine garden. Protecting his roses from frost or heat-waves. The first time she came to the house, he asked her to remove her shoes, before leading her into a cavernous room with dozens of antique globes, in the corner of which lived a sickly iguana named Leonardo.

Terrance told her he needed a gardening assistant for the roses and, in the spring and summer, a small veggie patch. He explained that his grandmother had been an avid rose grower, and that—with no discernible transition—as his grandmother's memory and dignity left her in old age, his step-uncle had abused her senility to molest him as a young boy in her house. When he was released from the spare room, his brain ringing, he would go out and see the roses, wilting or dead, and cry. Allowing such a miracle of nature to rot, he said, was a hideous crime. On her way out, with plans to return the following Tuesday, he mentioned that he too was a paedophile. He had been convicted for having great volumes of illegal material on his hard drive, but he was not, he said, practising. He hoped this would not affect her decision. She said nothing and returned the following week in overalls. She had not since seen the inside of his house.

Wednesdays and Fridays she left free for semi-regulars and new clients. These were the days that still most resembled that first job. She would watch men with erections, weeping. She dressed in scant clothes while being instructed on how to fix a car engine. She would sit in a cupboard or by a pool while a man rubbed his pants or talked of his mother. If no calls came, she clipped her nails and applied face masks or mopped her kitchen, ordering takeaway while bingeing sitcoms or docu-dramas. Sometimes she spent hours just scrolling through TikTok, watching women lacquer their nails in elaborate iridescent patterns, decorating each talon with diamonds or flowers or fruit skins before filing them off again. She watched other intricate fingers cut up bars of soap and paint their faces in multilayered rainbows or to resemble Disney princesses. She watched clips of women edited to change into twenty versions of the latest fashion so fast that no single outfit was decipherable. Sometimes they were dancing, each outfit changing at seamless sections of their bouncing routine. She wondered if they had jobs like hers. She wondered how long they spent on those twenty-second videos. She did not ever paint her nails. Sometimes she just sat on her back stoop, drinking tea, green or mushroom, looking out into the wilderness, listening to the calls of birds or shrieks of bats, gently hallucinating or growing tired, before she realised the time and went to bed.

Every second Saturday, she woke up at the crack of dawn and met a man who'd founded a successful pyramid scheme before he'd been charged with multiple counts of fraud, and then just as successfully avoided the accusations with expensive lawyers and a willingness to snitch on his business partner. He never told her this, but she remembered his trial on the news. He now called himself Jack, had grown a beard and dyed his hair chestnut brown. They would meet at the beginning of a hiking trail, Jack always ten minutes early, his fleece coat unzipped, performing Tai Chi in intense exhales. He would encourage her to hydrate, passing her a bottle of something called EverBrite or GroundedLite or MorningSite with indecipherable ingredients and long-passed expiry dates. There were many internet forums dedicated to the ways in which Jack had conned vulnerable people out of hundreds of thousands of dollars. They detailed their sons with Down syndrome now condemned to poverty, mothers who'd been robbed of a dignified end of life, and their own lost inheritance. The forums talked also of the women who'd worked for him, and just how much they were paid off to keep what he did to them out of the news cycle.

She and Jack walked for four to six hours, sometimes not talking at all, or commenting only on a tricky step or which fork to take. Mostly, however, Jack talked. He talked about chakras and the benefits of turmeric, the importance of antioxidants, about the universe and the universe's plan. In the four years since Jack had been her client, they had walked almost every path in the mountains and now redid old ones, remarking on the changes in route, large trees felled or fallen, a river that no longer ran through there.

Once, trekking through the burnt forest, the tree trunks spiralled in a green fuzz of epicormic growth, they saw a trail of carrots, the remnants of an air drop to feed wildlife. A few of the carrots were bitten to their nib, but most of them rotted on the recovering earth, black and spotted with saplings. In the early days of their walks, they'd seen birds and quolls and echidnas and koalas and kangaroos, and once, among a creek, a shy platypus. They often had to caution each other against snakes and spooked wombats, but each year these warnings came less and less, the mountains becoming quieter and quieter.

As if attuned to the volume of chatter, they regularly walked in silence now, broken only by a rendition of what Jack was grateful for that week, their cheeks and nose freezing to numbness. The woman at the local newsagent always winked at him, he was blessed to be on the receiving end of her boundless optimism. It was infectious, wasn't it? Watch that rock on your right, she said. Jack never requested she bare her breast or swim in the river naked, but during their walks she found herself fantasising of him telling her, in the same calm voice with which he talked about smoothie recipes or the benefits of rose quartz, just exactly what he would like to do to her, his neck muscles clenching.

On Sundays, she had family dinner. Her parents had long overcome the disappointment of her not going to university and instead accepted her vague explanations of running an online business. The new world, where you could earn a living from the comfort of your home, was beyond them. Her father specifically did not probe her, but her mother occasionally asked how it was going. Her brother was twenty and apparently knew what her line of work was, although he perhaps had her pinned as doing something that stemmed from grimy movies bathed in neon. When he was younger, he adored her, running to the door each afternoon from school with a drawing he'd made her. Now he sulked in his bedroom until dinner was served, then came out to eat and tell her she looked like a whore. Her father would yell at him to watch his manners, he would return to his bedroom, and after the meal she would watch whatever television her parents had lined up, her mother crocheting a blanket and attempting small talk about church or the school—she was a librarian— while her father sat there, clutching a mug of tea, his ears as red as if the sun were shining through them.

About once a month, on a day she did not have work, she would drive forty-five minutes southwest to meet a woman in her thirties who knitted her own clothes and used her own excrement to fertilise her garden. The woman slung a baby to one hip, supporting the child with one hand while she sold her a brown paper bag of psychedelic mushrooms with the other. The woman sometimes gave her mittens or a pumpkin, which she would take home and wear or make soup from. She had met this woman because her husband had once been a client. The woman talked often of the divine luck of meeting her husband, about the gruelling years it took to rescue him from his own personal darkness.

Years ago, she had taken the mushrooms only in micro-doses while she worked, then soon found herself micro-dosing all the time and taking enough to slip into vivid hallucinations while she was with clients. The mushrooms gave her a light, open feeling; she became a vessel in which to observe the world without judgement.

She continued to lovingly prune a rose bush while Terrance talked in equal measures of bygone French writers and how he wished he were able to visit a playground. Not, he assured her, to reach any sexual fulfilment, simply to observe children in flight. They were so filled with joy. He had considered, in the past, castration.

Interesting, she said, should she prune at the branch or further up the stem?

She learnt how to fold an origami flower, crane, box, frog, giraffe from the man who would not even give her a fake name. Sometimes, if she had made an incorrect fold or an object more beautiful than his own, he sat in silence staring at her for upwards of three minutes. She held his gaze and matched his breathing. She began to hum. She always left her origami on the table on the way out.

Her brother came over to her at the family dinner, leant down, and whispered in her ear that she had cum-breath.

How is uni going? she asked. Are you still enjoying your drama elective?

With Jack she walked around the only landscape she had ever known, bright and early in the morning, coming to an inner stillness. She could sometimes even see, among its dead or moist greenery, the animals that had once lived there, could make out the silhouette of a marsupial, the rising chorus of galahs, calling. Sometimes, instead, she saw the animals that would inhabit there in the future, in the flooded plains or dried desert, the micro fauna that would outlive them. She walked through the bush, felt its forestry shiver around her, crawling with organisms.

In late autumn, she got downstairs neighbours. She lived close to town in a small duplex, the downstairs of which had been empty for as long as she'd been there. They arrived one afternoon when she was drinking tea on her balcony at the rear. The woman, who looked to be around her own age, waved from her car as she unloaded boxes. A boy of eight or so got out of the backseat clutching a large plush toy to his chest. He walked straight up her back steps and held it above his head. It's a quokka, he told her.

Right, she said.

Lucas, said his mother, come on, buddy, what did we say about not invading people's personal space?

Aw, Lucas said. From two feet away he waved at her then retreated down the stairs.

Sorry, the woman called up.

It did not occur to her to help with the boxes and instead she sat there, clutching her tea, watching the both of them unpack. The car door morphed into the face of a lady she'd long accepted was God. She did not want to deal with Her right then, so she looked up to the sky, where God reconstructed Herself out of a constellation.

They're endangered because they trust people too much, the sky said.

Go away, she said.

No.

Leave me be, I'm drinking tea.

Leave me be, I'm drinking tea. Leave me be, I'm drinking tea. Leave me be, I'm drinking tea.

The day after she moved in, the woman knocked on her back door. She introduced herself as George and said again that she was sorry about Lucas, he didn't have a great radar for appropriate conduct. If you'd like, George said, you're welcome to join us for dinner tonight. She thanked the woman, but said she had work.

She did not in fact have work but that night she got ready to leave the house anyway, having realised that her footsteps upstairs, even muffled, would give her away, as would the presence of her car outside. Leaving her apartment, she surprised herself by turning and knocking on the downstairs door.

George said she'd had a feeling she'd show up, that she had plenty of soup on, come on in.

She sat down next to Lucas, who soon started a steady monologue on rockfish. George served soup and sat listening to her son in rapt attention.

It occurred to her that she should have brought something—a bottle of wine, some cheese. No sooner had she thought this than George produced a bottle of unlabelled red and two wineglasses, holding one up as a question. She nodded. In these situations, she thought, she was no better than Lucas. Aside from her mother, her interactions with other women were limited to shop staff and the occasional disembodied voice on her phone calling her a slut, or asking just who exactly this was. Usually, her clients who had wives or girlfriends were discreet, but every once in a while—she suspected when the client wanted out of a relationship—a phone would be left unattended and the women, rightly suspicious, would call. These women would be either eerily calm or hysterical. She would listen to their grievances, say politely that she thought they had the wrong number, then hang up and order herself a new phone.

Lucas whined when he finished dinner, but as soon as George told him it was time for bed, he took his plate to the sink and went to bathe. He reappeared briefly in worn flannel pyjamas, correctly buttoned, said goodnight, then went to his room. He was allowed fifteen minutes of reading before lights out, his mother called after him. Going to check on him, George came back declaring he was dead to the world and pulled out another bottle of wine.

George smiled at her. You're a hard one to crack, she said.

She asked George if she was a ballerina, and George laughed. That obvious, is it?

George looked like she should be modelling expensive watches or perfume in hard-to-reach parts of Europe. Her hair hung just past her chin and accentuated her cheekbones perfectly. She did not tell George this.

She had been, George told her, quite a good dancer once. But it becomes difficult to go on pointe when you're four months pregnant. Motherhood, she said, was much more rewarding. She took a sip of her wine. It was a miracle she got pregnant in the first place, she added, the diet she was on. George looked out the window. If, she said, you could call an eating disorder a diet.

There was a lull in conversation and then George asked her, So, what do you do then? She surprised herself again by telling George the truth. At least in part: she helped people, she said.

Oh, like a social worker?

Not quite, she said. Then: Men, mostly.

Oh. George broke into a wide grin. She understood—her husband would have liked her. She said this matter-of-factly, without bitterness.

Where is he?

Off with the other woman.

Oh. Well, she said just to say something, he probably would like me.

George looked mortified and then burst into laughter.

Her life continued: Winter setting in meant her walks with Jack were cancelled or postponed with more frequency. Sometimes she went anyway; either the weather cleared up at the last minute or she got steadily soaked and developed a cold. The old man who sat in front of his television started taking a regimented and complicated rotation of medicine. She spent an extra half-hour making sure his pills went into the correct slots in his dispenser. Each evening she called to check he'd taken them.

She continued to garden at Terrance's and developed hard callouses, small cuts where the rose thorns bit her. She turned up to see the origami man one morning and discovered an empty site. A new regular, a young man with cystic acne, filled the Monday-morning spot. He was afraid, he said, he'd nurtured a porn addiction. He could no longer see women as people. He just wanted to talk, nothing more. He would like to have a girlfriend but did not, he said, have the kind of personality girls wanted to hang out with. She saw him for breakfast at expensive cafes or went bowling with him. He talked about movies and books and what he did or didn't like about them. Once in a while, his face would contort with rage and he'd call her a fucking worthless piece of shit. He hoped she choked on a dick and died. Then it would pass, his face would slacken. Sorry, he'd say, he was so sorry, he couldn't help it. Other times he talked of his latest porn-hole, the increasingly fetishist nature of his searches, his inability to get a hard-on, the overwhelming feelings of numbness that crept in, earlier and earlier each day.

At least twice a week, she went downstairs to George's. George was an excellent cook and Lucas a mature eater. He ate the same curry or eggplant risotto they did. After he went to bed, George would talk about her life in Sydney, the muscles she'd pulled, a teacher at Lucas's school who hated her. In return, she would tell George small details here and there, about her life, her day, and sometimes her clients. Nothing, she told herself, that would break her self-imposed code of client confidentiality. George would shriek with laughter or say she had to be fucking joking, but never looked at her with pity.

On her days off she sometimes babysat Lucas. When George tried to pay her, she refused. These were some of the rare occasions she was not on mushrooms. She could not always predict them, though, and there were times when George rushed up the stairs to ask if she was free for a couple of hours, she'd been asked to cover a shift—George had picked up a job as a yoga instructor—and there was not much she could do about the low-level hum, her pupils dilating, the world expanding.

She wanted Lucas to remind her of her younger brother, but he did not. In his youth her brother had been sporty and artistic, had taken easily to other children and enjoyed creating convoluted storylines where only his special ability could save the day. Lucas liked to sit in silence, his encyclopedia of animals open on his knees. When he was done, he would wait by her silently until she noticed him, at which point he would report what he'd just read, almost word-for-word.

One day, she came back from gardening and went to sit on her back balcony. The dirt on her arms looked to be making a pattern, the veins underneath her skin rippling in mimicry of it. George was squatting in the backyard, inspecting something in the grass.

She looked down and almost cried out in fright; the top half of Lucas's head peeked up over the balcony. He was standing on the bin below, hands clinging to the rail. Christ, she said, be careful.

Did she know, he said, orchid mantis could make themselves look like orchids? That's why they're called orchid mantises.

No, she said, she didn't know that.

Do you think that's what happened to all the animals?

What?

Do you think they're pretending to be flowers?

Oh, she said, sure.

A bird made from yellow roses appeared at his shoulder; it yawned at her sceptically.

Really? he said.

She felt a buzz, like the back of her skull was opening. She thought of the constant rustle that had always been there in the background, the soundtrack of her life. She looked down at George and saw her reach a hand to her sternum, absent-mindedly, as if to fiddle with a necklace. She imagined the things that ran and leaped, made the landscape shriek and murmur—the wildlife increasingly scattered across the shape of the mountains. George frowned, then looked down at her bare neckline.

Sure, she said again. Maybe, she said, probably not.

Preparation

♥ liked by treesglobal and 3123 others

I guess you could say I'm a citizen of the world. I mean, sure, I was born in Randwick Royal Women's Hospital and the past twenty-six years of my life I have 'resided' in the suburb of Coogee Bay, but I like to think I'm globalised. I've travelled, I'm cultured, my favourite still water is imported from Finland.

My travels started with a whirlwind trip to Europe for my eighteenth birthday. And I do mean whirlwind— some of the countries blurred together a bit. At one point when I was on the plane, asleep against the window, snoring with my mouth open, eye mask on—$39, organic, locally sourced silk—the whole of Austria just slipped under my window. Bethany and the hostess apparently found it hilarious.

This was all before I knew about how bad flying is for the environment. Before I began to think about my place in the world and started #project-plastic. Bethany's dad loaned us the jet and we pretty much just flew anywhere and everywhere. Don't blame me! You make some friends in high school, you just want to fit in, the popular girls turn out to have billionaire business-mogul fathers. Or mothers, it's 2019. I don't make the rules.

Look—I don't travel in jets anymore. I mean, I do take planes sometimes. I live in Australia, a giant island in the middle of nowhere. Can you imagine? How else am I meant to get around? Don't say on a boat! One morally bankrupt issue at a time!

♥ liked by beam_me_up and 2044 others

I've finally got my jar! As I've begun to follow more ethically likeminded people, who've also been monitoring their use of plastic, I've noticed a lot of them keep all the plastic they can't avoid or recycle in a jar.

I went on a hunt for a jar that suits me, and I found it. It's already pretty full #yikes.

♥ liked by greenmum74 and 2678 others

Before I began my #wellness-journey, I was travelled but I wasn't *worldly.* Now, though? Even as I write this, my pants: ethical linen woven in Ontario. Shirt? Made in a women's prison in Saigon. Slippers? New Zealand sheep's wool. My glasses are responsibly sourced Galapagos tortoiseshell. Even my hair dye is made from Indigenous red rocks from the Kimberley.

Now I don't have to travel the world—the world travels to me. If you went through my house, you'd find something from every corner. Even the ocean. *Especially* the ocean. The bag I've been using is a limited-edition design of recycled plastic from the deepest part of the Pacific explored by man.

♥ liked by lilag and 1004 others

As you guys know, me and Bethany aren't friends anymore. I've seen the light; she unfollowed me on every platform. I refuse to feel bad about that part of my life.

♥ liked by jorgef and 785 others

In my previous life, I travelled to a lot of places: America, Europe, the Netherlands, Japan, Spain. Recently, however, as I've been staying home and focusing on my #projectplastic, I've had time to think about things. And on reflection, most of the places I travelled to were for work.

What I'm saying is I didn't really spend time outside of OECD nations. Unless you count the seventeen-hour layover I spent sleeping under a row of chairs in an Indian airport. And Bali a handful of times. Even I need a place to unwind. Sometimes you've just got to relax, put a blue-light filter on your phone, limit your posts to once a day, get fully into some morning yoga, and just #reload.

♥ liked by ecobitch and 683 others

Last time I went to Bali, I met Pip at a silent retreat. Pip is my new friend. She lives in Sydney too. She's from the western suburbs. She rides her bike everywhere, grows her own vegetables, and has a HECS debt. Sometimes she doesn't go on Instagram for days at a time. She says things like: 'I don't think you're properly considering your privilege.' Pip makes me a better person. I've had some major breakthroughs with Pip. Epiphanies, even. She's been making me think more deeply about the world around me, and I've started to realise how much I really don't know—and how much more there is to do to truly live #sustainably.

I've also started seeing a therapist; it's all because of her. It's good to have a friend who's more compatible with your lifestyle.

♥ liked by piploves and 459 others

Look, I'm not saying there aren't people out there with bigger issues than me. Pip has been telling me a lot about climate refugees and corporate pollution, so I want to

acknowledge that I live a fairly privileged life. However, there is real pressure when all these people you don't know care about what you say and do and look like. Sometimes, as I've been moving towards a lifestyle focused on #community, #sustainability, and #wellness, it's become overwhelming. It's got to a point where I'll just be minding my own business, researching brands or healthy smoothies, going about my life, and then it will hit me. Yesterday, I was scrolling through my feed and I started to think about all the things that could go wrong. About how I have so much power with this one thing, but yet, beyond it, I have none at all. No life skills whatsoever. Nada. I started to panic, my hands froze up and I couldn't speak.

I'm feeling better but I still feel anxious. I mean, what if I said or did the wrong thing and everyone turned on me? It would all be gone. All of it. I don't have billionaire parents.

♥ liked by plantminded and 849 others

So I've had to get a new jar. I'm working out a solution. I've started to think more critically about the stuff I'm promoting on here. I deleted some old posts and lost a bunch of followers.

I have worked to change my content, but the truth is, even the ethically made products being sent to me, bamboo bras and bamboo toothbrushes and bamboo face washers—a whole lot of bamboo really—is still sent in plastic. Not all of it, because obviously these brands are also trying their best. But it's got me thinking about how hard it is to be sustainable in an unsustainable world. And I mean, what

about all the postage? Isn't that just as bad as travelling? Does that count towards my ecological footprint or to the companies' that send me stuff? Sometimes I just want to get on the next plane to the Mediterranean, sit in the sun and forget completely about the whole world-is-on-fire issue. The point being that I had to get a bigger jar, which, to be honest, is already full.

♥ liked by medifaith and 432 others

My therapist says my way of immediately monetising genuine experiences is a product of an unhealthy relationship with my phone. I'm working on it. At the moment, I'm taking afternoon walks down to the beach just to go outside and be in nature. Right now, I have to go completely without my phone. Walking along and down the cliffs, seeing the blue sea and feeling crisp spring air—and all these dogs at the park—it's all too beautiful and tempting, so the phone is staying at home.

♥ liked by quitesaige and 480 others

I know the whole point of my walks down to the beach without my phone is to reflect on my place in the world and how I could move forward ethically. But the truth is, all I could think about at first was how I wished I had my phone. More recently, as I've started to look around and think logistically about taking a picture down at the beach, I've thought how it's not even really that Instagrammable. Because what they don't tell you is how much cleaning up of places you have to do if you want a decent photo. And all along the cliffs here, down the path, around the crescent of sand along the beach, all the way to the north side where teenagers jump off the cliffs into the water at high tide, where I saw a shy octopus once, black tentacles burrowing into the sand—it's all filled with rubbish.

I've started to bring a bag on my walks in the morning, to pick up all the rubbish I see. I'm going to have to get more jars. I'm going to have to rethink things.

♥ liked by fruitnat and 959 others

So since I began picking up rubbish on my walks, now whenever I'm out in the world posting, as I've cleaned up my surroundings, I ask myself if this water bottle I'm moving to take a nice picture in the park is my responsibility. Like, was the trash I was moving to benefit me, my rubbish? And then I thought, if I've touched it, it probably is my rubbish. So I'd take it home and put it in the jars—I've had to get more jars, because the big jar filled up even quicker than the small jar with all the rubbish I've been picking up on my walks. If I go on like this the whole house will be filled with jars of rubbish. But I mean, if I think about it, isn't my house just a big jar anyway? A big jar that contains me?

♥ liked by givemore and 845 others

#projectplastic is evolving. It started with the living room. I pasted all the plastic from my jars onto my walls, and within a day I'd wallpapered the room in this bright collage of chip packets and beer labels, those little sushi fish and even condom wrappers. My arms hurt!

♥ liked by lukas_g and 792 others

I thought it would take forever, doing the whole house, but before I knew it the floor and ceilings were done, then the kitchen, then the bathroom, then the spare room, then my room.

Now I've started on the fixtures, pasting films of plastic on the sinks, taps, lampshades. Finding a piece of the right size and texture—it's like doing a giant puzzle with no reference picture. There's no cheating; only I know there's a salt-and-vinegar chip packet in one of these jars that will fit the gap on the outside of the toilet bowl, wrapping perfectly to its curve.

♥ liked by marxistvegan and 843 others

Pip brought her friends over to look at the house, and a few of them think I'm an artist. This one lanky guy wearing sandals and socks called Grisham told me I should have a night where I open my house up, like an exhibition, and have people come over to look at my plastic-rubbish home, but later I learnt he washes his hair with beer, so I don't know.

♥ liked by tasmin and 301 others

Today I started with the outside—this is what I do now. Every day, I take a bag to the beach, I fill the bag up, I come home, I wash the plastic, then I paste it to my walls. If I can, in the evening I go for another walk. Yesterday I didn't even think about taking my phone, I just started walking and picking up rubbish. Soon I'll start on another layer.

♥ liked by green4ella and 673 others

I thought that coating my house in plastic would make me feel trapped, like how I feel with this job sometimes. Not that I don't appreciate you guys, it's just sometimes I feel like, if I don't post I don't get paid, so I'd have to find another job, and realistically, do I even have any skills outside this job? I said to my therapist how I wondered if I was subconsciously making my own jail, but actually it's done the opposite, coating my house in plastic. It feels like a way out.

Apparently I'm the street eccentric. People walk up from the beach to come stare at the house. School kids take detours to look at it, loitering in the driveway until I wave at them and they run off snickering. Anthony, the neighbour's kid, came over and asked what I was doing and I said coating my house in plastic, then he grabbed a pasting brush and climbed up the ladder. His parents don't mind. Anything to get him out of the house, it seems.

♥ liked by enviro_mntl and 211 others

The roof is done now. In the sun it's glossy and hot. The first wave of summer heat came last week and thick steam rose off the roof and distorted the air around it. You'd think it'd be hot inside but it's nice and insulated, and when I open the widow at night the wind whips through the house and whistles gently against the plastic. It's like falling asleep in a giant seashell.

♥ liked by koalaty and 356 others

Another good thing that's come out of all this is I'm spending time with Anthony who is really into a video game called Red Dead Redemption, and is definitely the kind of kid I made fun of—well, bullied—in high school. Not that I don't make fun of him a little now. I mean, he's a really bad swimmer (even though he's lived about 100 metres from a famously swimmable—from *the* famously swimmable—beach his whole life), his knees are comically knobbly, and when we went for a walk to get plastic and ran into a girl in his music class, his voice did that embarrassing drop-lift-drop thing puberty does to it, so it's hard not to tease him. I think it's good for him, though. He's learning how to loosen up. Mainly, though, I think he's good for me. He's made me think more about my past self. Not about my environmental ignorance, more how I treated and expected to be treated by other people. I'm not really sure where to go from here but I'm asking myself questions, for sure.

♥ liked by gothecology and 202 others

Now that everything is coated I've begun making new stuff out of plastic. Grisham, Pip and Anthony helped me make a chicken coop. They keep asking me if I'll open the house to the public. I said I think I'm on display enough, but you never know. Then Grisham asked me what I thought I did

all this for and I didn't have an answer.

What should I call my chickens?

♥ liked by juliaglobal and 798 others

Okay, I'm doing it! Open house tomorrow night, address closer to the time. Everyone who wants to come should bring some rubbish to contribute to the house!

♥ liked by sheeva and 489 others

Thanks everyone who came out! It was a really good night. Thanks to those of you who brought something for the project! Some of you brought nostalgic stuff (thank you for the He-Man figurine) and a little too many of you brought expired condoms, but

I appreciate it anyway. I still don't have a very good answer about why I do any of this (thanks Grisham for asking me in front of everyone), but seeing so many people come together is a pretty good result. Anthony came and didn't even blush when I made fun of how pasty he is, Pip wrote a poem and shared it with everyone, and so many of you talked to me about future collaborations. Who knows what the future holds. But for now it's been nice to #giveback.

♥ liked by barbiehurl and 1305 others

It's weird, I noticed just now that in my living room, where I first started, in parts where all the layers of plastic are clear, the wall underneath has started to crumble. All around the house I could find tiny see-through holes and it looks sweaty underneath, like the house is under pressure. Then I went to my kitchen window and looked out at the ocean. In the distance, a big wave swelled. I got this metallic taste in my mouth and then I thought how maybe this was all just a sort of preparation. I began to imagine how, years from now, when the wind has eroded the cliffs, and water's flooded the bay, the house walls will disintegrate, but its plastic moulding will still be there. Erect and shiny, like a cicada shell.

Intermission II:
On the Mythology in the Room
(Field Notes)

Well. Where to even begin? There's Agatha of course, she's been around since—well, since forever. No one really knows. She used to be more elusive, I suppose, but you could always find her if you wandered into the woods alone. Fleeing something in a fit of terror, usually. You need to be either running away from your destiny or a lost and distraught child. As long as you aren't actually looking for her, easy as. Oh, sometimes a bunch of misfits can find her if they've got a dare about which one can get the closest to her house. Yes, you can definitely find her in the woods, but also sometimes in the decrepit house at the end of your street, maybe in a cave by the sea somewhere. Oh, and that extra stop on the elevator—the one you've never seen before despite working at the same place for how long—she'll be there. Definitely. She can surprise you. There've been rumours of course, over the years. That there are three of her. Not true, not at all. Other times they say she's got a coven, but you can hardly expect her to have gone around all these years without any friends. There was that time everyone was claiming she was fattening kids up to eat them. Luring them into the woods with candy. Total slander.

A lot of people, when they do see her, run away screaming. Just at the sight of her, imagine. Imagine if someone came into your house uninvited—if they broke into your house—and then fled at the sight of you. Used to upset her a lot, but she's got tough skin. Literally! Ha. Oh, that was in bad taste, don't tell her I said that. I feel awful. Well, she's much better now, much older, wiser. She's gone by a lot of names over the years, old Aggy. A lot of names, a lot of faces. Sometimes she's beautiful but usually she's, well, like I said, with the fleeing in horror. Sometimes warts, sometimes a big nose, sometimes she's green! Other times her eyes are opaque and she rolls them around a lot, which is like—okay, take it down a peg, you know? When she is beautiful, it's the type of beauty that comes with whispers of evil incarnate, you get it. Seduce your husband, kill the king. She can't win. Either way she's THE symbol of women without the influence of men. Used to be a bad thing. People are pretty into it now, though. She loves it.

There *are* others of course. A lot of them got burnt, although we don't really like to talk about that. Tough period. People once believed in all this stuff a lot more than they do now; hell, I reckon a lot of these things came out of that period. But you know, it was a lot of grief, dealing with it all. All the superstition. They don't call it the Dark Ages for nothing. But Agatha, she's where it all started. Hilarious woman, got some stories. If you do meet her, tell her I sent you. Might change your luck. You never know what you're going to get with her. Impossible to say if she'll help you or make everything a whole lot worse. Nothing personal, depends on her mood. She does mess with people just for fun sometimes, which I admit isn't great for PR. But look, I understand, I'd get bored too.

Oh Christ, we need to move on. This way please. Right so, let's go down near the water. Come on people, we haven't got all day.

There now. Water has been, historically, pretty loaded with meaning and metaphor, ripe for tales from all corners. A *body* of water. And who is, historically, a body? Exactly. Sailors would claim to fall in love with the sea. Their boats were also typically *she/hers*. Honestly. Men. But I suppose I'd be out of a job without them, wouldn't I? Ha, oh sorry to those of you who brought one here today; no need to worry, you can pick them up on the way out. There're a few sea witches of course, but we spent so much time on Agatha, I think you get the gist. Ah okay, here they are. Mermaids. There might be one or two selkies around as well. Yes, over there. Or maybe they're just seals? I can never tell the difference. Apparently there's a trick to it, but anyway, look, they all do a variant on the same thing. Do not listen to them! If they start to sing. Comprehende? And be very careful with the little one you've got there—how cute! Not a man yet, are you sweetie? But really, do be careful. Just keep an eye on him. In fact let's just put our earplugs in before we go have a closer look.

Great. That was good, wasn't it? You had fun, didn't you little man? Yes they are fun to play with, I know, they seem nice. Some of them, all they really want is a good chat but you can't risk it. They're meant to just get sailors, and they do. Well, they did. And they were happy doing that for yonks, but mostly these days the only sailors left are in giant commercial fishing trawlers. The girls lost a few friends to the nets. Once they're on the boats they can't do much. And mind you, those at sea aren't as romantic as they used to be. So yeah, look, a lot of different factors, but essentially they've been known to snatch a local, is what I'm saying. Some of the nasty ones do it for sport. See that girl with the teeth and the seaweed for hair? On the rock on the far side? Stay away from her. Trust me. Best not to mention the redhead around them too. Upsets them. Grief, mostly, but a few of them are jealous. Notoriety, see.

Okay. Alright, this way, this way. While we're on the move let's talk symbolism. Agatha, again, is responsible for a lot of it. Cats, frogs, bats. All illusions to female empowerment and therefore considered omens. I know, right. Groan. And then there is the—hmm, how to say? Symbolism for the *origin of our powers*. Pardon me. The cowrie shell was the go-to, back in the day. A bit on the nose, if you ask me. Then flowers, flowers are still popular. Lotuses specifically. Can anyone think of anything else? Fruit! Yes, fruit's a good one. Pomegranates, pawpaw, anything these days—but then we'd have to get into modern art, I'm thinking we don't have time for that.

Apples! Yes, well. Corruption in the garden. Fertility. The root of all evil. Yada yada. You got me: we'll circle back to that later.

Well, yes of course the barbie doll plays a part in it, not so much anymore, but there's a whole department on Beauty Standards (BS, we call it). They're all stressed to the nines at the moment. The amount of content coming out every day. I think we should just drop the whole thing—it's a relic of the past. It used to be a fairly manageable office, half a dozen people figuring out the distortion of the ribs caused by the corset. Now it's a whole building, staff running around like headless chooks. People thought with the whole liberation thing it would get easier, and now with gender roles, gender itself, being deconstructed more and more—we thought it would be way easier. And in some ways that's true, but you could also argue that it's much more complicated. I saw someone have a breakdown because they couldn't figure out if lips should be matt or glossy. Best to avoid them. This way.

Right, where are we? Dark alleyway on a moonless night. Right, yes. Stay together please. Stay on this side of the road, we're going to approach the bridge but not actually go under it. There's one of them. There, under the light. Tall, pale brunette. With the stare and the lipstick and the dramatic widow's peak. You'll be fine with her, unless you're a predator yourself. Let's stay here anyway, we don't want to talk to her. Gives me the heebie jeebies. She's been around forever, or people like her, maybe as long as Agatha. Apparently she claims to have stood still for so long she can feel the earth's rotation around the sun, can feel the axis tilt in space. Bullshit if you ask me—excuse my language. Always trying to mess with you. Always the same. She's got a few of her kind, men and non-binary folk too, but she's a specific type, this one. See how she's waiting outside a pub? See the back door there? I bet she saw some guy do something horrible to a girl and now she's waiting. It's a lot harder for them these days, most places it's difficult to get away with murder, and there are too many diseases now. Most of them stay out of overdeveloped countries. Can't keep up with the technology. Much better to be the legend in the Amazon, the rumour in the village, than the front page of national news.

Oh, here he comes now. See that guy who's come out to take a piss by the bin? Yes, there she goes. Let's get a move on. Hurry. Nobody wants to see this part. Blood makes me queasy.

I feel like we've lingered a lot on the negatives. On the vixens, and the red and black, the cursed and such. Let's consider the other side. The Madonnas. Symbols of purity.

Nothing? Well, sure, there're a lot fewer of them. The lotus we already touched on, but in some cultures it symbolises the, erm, unsullied. Virginity. Purity and all that's holy. What else? Often there's a lot of blonde hair and white dresses, sometimes hair so blonde and long it can be thrown down as a rope. Damsels in distresses; please save me, dear prince, et cetera. A lot of the time we're sleeping under a glass coffin for some reason when Prince Charming comes along. That's always creeped me out. Then there're the roses. I mean, what doesn't the rose symbolise? Precisely.

Sometimes we need saving from dragons, evil witches, that kind of thing. Sometimes we're unfairly captive, sometimes we've pricked our finger and fallen asleep. There's the red again. Drops of blood, you get it. Red Riding Hood—although I've never really figured out what the red in that story is about. Other times we turn into swans at night—white swans, you get me. Whatever, we generally need to be saved, whether that be by waking us up or breaking a transformation curse, and in order for that to happen we need? Right: our true love's kiss. Pretty standard practice.

There was that one time where we did the turning—frog into a prince. There was a lot of frog kissing after that. Useless and very unhygienic. A gateway to toads, and that's a rabbit hole you don't want to go down. Then what? Come on people, think.

Fairy godmothers! Right, yes. Let's go find them up here. Should be just around the corner. Ah, here we go. See this clearing here with all the sunshine and birds tweeting? There they are! Notice the colourful dresses and the wands and the incessant singing and the white horse passing through the woods in the background? That sort of thing happens all the time here. I think that one is picking flowers, Jesus. Look—wonderful ladies. Good, yes, but usually sexless. And a bit picky themselves, not that you heard that from me. Tend to only help a certain type. That glass-slipper girl? I mean, she's lovely, but a bit dull is all I'm saying.

Right, we really do have to wrap things up here, so let's think. There's light and dark, good and bad. Usually depending on how agreeable we have or have not been to the men in our life, you get me. A bit didactic, but that's the business. There *is* Medusa— scorned woman who turns men into stone. She's a hoot, but we'd have to get into the Greek stuff and frankly that's not my area of expertise.

She-wolves, yes. Sometimes we fully transform into wolves at will, sometimes we're cursed into the body of a wolf until we've repaid our debt or whatever. There've been many sightings over the years. Sometimes it's just a woman who hasn't shaved. The '70s were a nightmare, phones off the hook.

Oh, before I forget, see these mushrooms here? If you ever see them outside, turn around. Run the other way. Actually, let's just all do that now. Quickly.

Okay, we've all caught our breath. Look, it was the right thing to do. Saved you a headache. They might be hard to spot, those mushrooms, if you're out in the woods and such, but if you see them in your kitchen or at the train station? Get out.

Call a cleaner, walk to the next stop. Nothing overly bad will happen, it's just fairies. They actually have nothing to do with us, sometimes they just come in from the general myth department, cross-contamination. A pain in the arse. If you *must* follow the mushrooms, or you don't see them or whatever, you've got to do exactly what the fairies say. *Exactly* what they say. Real micro-managers, if you ask me. Whatever they promise you, they're just looking for a loophole, understand?

I guess we're coming to the end, so I've got to go into the one thing we're all avoiding. We've been talking round them all morning. That's right: stepmothers. Which is—look there's a lot. Sometimes it's not all their fault. Impossible standards left by the dead mother, a whole heap of hostility towards them before they even get properly into their role. And they're human and therefore flawed, so there's that. Well, most of them are human. They have a union of course. Claim to be unfairly vilified. But a lot of the time, *a lot of the time,* you have to admit they do seem somewhat guilty, and some of them are downright evil. Here's their meeting room. They've asked me to ask you all if you'll sign their petition. No takers? Shocking. So I suppose this is where the apple comes in again. That whole thing with the hunter and the poison and the mirror? Dressing up a like a hag? Witchcraft? A Fiasco. *Fiasco.* A lot of the work the union does is trying to recover from that, optics-wise. Only so much you can do, though.

Right, I think that's about it for the day. Oh Christ, before I forget, you can pick up any men you brought with you at the front desk, where you can also validate your parking. You're welcome to grab a complimentary apple on the way out. Anyway, I'm sure there's more I've forgotten. I always forget something, there's so much here, more than I can possibly remember, but that's all we've got time for today. Shoot—yes, I can see the next group in the lobby. The main point of the session, really, was just trying to lay the groundwork. The basis for understanding all the symbols and meanings we've taken into our bodies. What we have to navigate in the world. But can you see it? How we've been written? Can you see us through time?

Fertile Soil

Summer had come and with it some strange encounters around the city. At work, or at conferences, on the train, in the corridors before my night class, strangers would greet me, asking after me like a long lost cousin. One week, an old man at the library said I was looking healthy and asked how I was settling in, and the next day a woman running down the street with a lapel bouncing off her sternum and a fitted skirt stopped when she saw me. She told me she couldn't stop, she was running late, but we'd catch up soon, then she took a large bite of the wrap she was clutching and cried, God, the chicken is so dry! Don't go to that cafe! And ran off again as best she could with the top half of her legs shellacked together. That same afternoon, what looked like two university students on the opposite platform waved with an enthusiasm I thought was passé for young people. I looked around to check no one was behind me, then turned hoping to get a better look at them, but a train pulled up, obscuring their particulars, and when it passed they were gone.

This is how these sort of things went down. Never wanting to be rude when I encountered these people, I met them with the same level of familiarity, asking how they were, what they'd been up to, agreeing, in our sweaty, soiled clothes, how oppressive the humidity was, swearing that the summers were getting worse, and of course they were.

Once, at a dinner party, I was having a lovely conversation with a young man—which is to say younger than me, although I am not old myself—only to realise he thought we'd met before. He offered me a glass of wine made from a variety of grape that was, he told me, found only in one village in Chile. I took the wine gladly, it was dry and delicious, and he began describing a tree that was growing in the front yard of the house we were in. He asked me first if I'd noticed the tree and if I knew what it was, and when I didn't he told me that it had been brought here on the First Fleet. There were, he said, eleven ships in the First Fleet, including three store ships of food, botanicals and animals—horses, cows, sheep and other ungulates that would decimate the soil and understorey on the continent. He began to explain the nature of the tree, how it needed more consistent and sparse rain, and a crisper atmosphere; how, in its upkeep, the plant took up a much larger quantity of resources than needed in its indigenous circumstances, and was most probably responsible for the destruction of many native species itself. But, after decades as an invasive species, he said, the tree had naturalised. It had, he said, even adapted to the subtropical summer floods and dry soil in the north half of the country we occupied—soil sapped of nutrients by the very sort of plants and animals he was talking about. Did I know this?

When I said I did not know this, he nodded solemnly and looked out the window.

I became suddenly self-conscious of the food I'd eaten that day, fish that was not caught locally and a strange sort of broccoli my husband found at a supermarket that looked like an acid trip. I thought of this food and retroactively stepped my way through the process of it being farmed and packaged and distributed to me, and on top of this an image become superimposed: a vision of the view from my kitchen window, of the mango tree in the backyard, sunburnt fruit rotten on the ground, seeds that fruit bats, shrieking in gluttonous delight, had discarded in the night.

How do you think, he said, we are supposed to become naturalised? I didn't answer as I didn't know what to say, so I stood there staring out the window. He shook his head as if waking himself from a daze and said, but I have not shown you what I've been working on, and pulled out his phone. He began to flip through pictures of large metal sculptures that appeared, despite their obvious solidness, to be moving, their shining surfaces undulating. At once resembling a tree or bush and then a wave cresting, a speaker throbbing, a body trying to escape—his body, it looked like, his beard, nose, a bouquet of elbows. They were round organic shapes, appearing completely smooth, without hinges or corners. I hope, he said, this will explain my absence from this sort of thing in the future. He would like to be working on it right now, but Reilly—Reilly was our host—had made him come. He pouted, and I don't think it was an affectation; he seemed unaware of how childish it made him look. I laughed and he smiled at me, inquisitive, keen to get in on the joke. But I only laughed again and asked what his sculpture meant.

That's just the thing, he said, at first he didn't know. For the longest time, he had been feeling something—a dread that came to him, in the middle of autumn. He paused and looked unsure how to go on. I am unsure how to go on, he said. It was like some sort of melancholy, from nowhere. He knew he was falling into depression but didn't know why. His life was going as well as it could have been, he had not been going through a breakup or some other personal tectonic shift—he did not feel trapped or stale in routine or anything. One day, he simply lost the will to live. He tried, he said, very hard to both stop this depression and to identify its cause. He exercised with more vigour, ate only the freshest organic food and began to see a therapist, a sort of stern hippie, he said, who prescribed a robust course of treatment. He once woke sodden at the end of a session of hypnotherapy to be reassured that it was perfectly normal, that's why there were plastic covers on the chairs. He grinned. He had pissed himself, everywhere, he said, everywhere. He walked home with his socks squelching with piss. He'd had to buy new shoes, he said, pointing. The shoes he was wearing did look very new. But still, he said, nothing. Nothing? I said. You didn't find out why you pissed yourself? Oh, he said, he'd drunk two litres of coconut water before the session. It wasn't, he continued, until his mother called him to wish him a happy birthday, and as an afterthought said he'd reached the age his father had been when he died.

A coolness spread through my mouth, although whether it was the Chilean wine or sadness for that young man, I didn't know. I attempted to say with a straight voice, without making his grief mine, I was sorry for his loss, but he waved me off, and said, flippantly, so that's what it's been about. Pardon? I asked. He spun his hand around, as if I had failed to grasp some mechanics he was explaining: my work, he said. Oh, I said, you are mourning your father. No, he said, I have been trying to forgive him. But wait—he said this as if remembering something urgent—you won't say I showed them to you, will you? The photos. Reilly would be mad at me, something about an embargo for the exhibition. Of course not, I said, and asked him when his exhibition was. Two months away, you will come, won't you? I nodded, smiled. It fell silent between us while he poured himself a glass of wine, and I asked him to forgive me, but what was his name?

At this point the young man looked up from his pouring, for a second I saw his face: devastated. But we've met, he said, as his wineglass filled to the brim. I thought, he said—but he'd overpoured, and, although I tried to apologise, I saw that tears had welled in the corners of his eyes. He then, realising that wine had dribbled down his pants and spotted onto the floor, said, oh god, what a mess, and ran off. He went not in the direction of the kitchen, but the front door, and I didn't see the young man again.

It was instances like this that brought on me a peculiar feeling, or dawning, of erasure, as if the city were conspiring against me. As if the weather, threatening forty degrees for three weeks without reprieve, had produced a form of heatstroke that affected my short-term memory. My connections to other people seemed tenuous, began to make less and less sense. For days I fretted over what was causing me to forget so many people. What had happened that I couldn't remember having previously met that sensitive young man? Why had I forgotten the life details of acquaintances, and sometimes the acquaintances themselves? And still the encounters went on: an old friend texted to say it was lovely running into me, my doctor told me I was already up to date with my pap smear, and when I went into a bookstore on a whim one afternoon, the bookseller smiled and said, back so soon.

I began to fear I was developing early-onset Alzheimer's, until that afternoon at a barbecue when I saw her, chest heaving, rummaging through a backpack. As most parties are in summer, in the culmination of the year, alcoholism ran rampant, and the day-to-day obligations of routine, of work, of exercise, of appointments, were discarded for the condensation collecting on the outside of a bottle. The time of year when the sun goes down but the heat never lets up, nor the mosquitoes. The days bleed one day into the next, morphing into one another. Which is to say, I cannot pinpoint now, precisely, which door it was. Which party, or whose house I was in when the doorbell rang.

I was the only person in the kitchen, all the other guests had retreated to the back deck. I opened the catch and knew immediately, in a sigh of relief, it was not me, but the young man and many other strangers like him that were mistaken. I greeted myself with a small smile.

I worried then that I'd perhaps ruined a budding romance between the artist and the woman who stood before me.

Hi—urgh, she said, sorry, she was just looking for the wine she brought. I know it's in here, she said. She walked in while still looking through her backpack, dropping the helmet under her arm. Shit, she said. I leant over to scoop it up and hand it to her; she looked up briefly and smiled. Thank you, she said, oh, there it—but then she looked back up, processing the information of my face.

I smiled and she laughed nervously. Oh wow, she said. We stood there staring at one another.

Everyone is on the deck, I said, if you want to . . .

Yes, she said. I suppose we should do that.

Here, let me. I reached out for the bottle and she handed me her helmet.

Oh no, she said, I meant, and she swapped the two objects and laughed again. Okay, out on the deck.

On our way through the kitchen she dumped her backpack on a stool.

What's your name? I said.

Anna.

Oh god—

It's short for Breanna, if that helps.

It did. I said, mine's not short for anything. Once we were outside the hosts said, ah! Anna, you're here, and hugged her.

My husband had not come to the barbecue and I never told him—I didn't know how to tell him—about Anna. Which is to say I don't know precisely when, or if, he knew there were two of us. Although we live in a small city, and therefore nothing stays a secret long. I can guess he heard strange rumours, but it's equally likely that he met her in much the same fashion I did, in that part of the summer, the sun sinking perpetually over another tsk of a beer opening. I have wondered, since I moved inland, west, up the Great Dividing Range to a city isolated by its landscape, what it was like when he met her. Did he mistake her for me on his first encounter? Greet her with a hug and say, you decided to come! She, in politeness, going along with it? Or did he do a doubletake and laugh nervously, as she had with me?

Perhaps he was not even sure when that first encounter was, and in any case our replacement was smooth—hinge-less, like the young man's sculptures. I do not know specifically when, but I am certain in the kitchen that morning, he thought she was me.

The day after the barbecue I called my mother, who seemed worried I was experiencing a breakdown and assured me that she had 'flesh birthed' me, and there was definitely no other baby involved. She offered to send me a recording of the birth, and then became offended when I declined. But, she said, she'd just had it digitised. Birthing, she said, is the closest thing we can experience to magic in this day and age, where technology has weeded the mystical out. She then described to me the precise contents of her lunch—a banana smoothie and an egg sandwich made with wholegrain bread she'd baked that morning. Which reminded her—the egg sandwich—of the texture of my placenta. Her placenta, our placenta, she said, which she'd eaten shortly after my birth. Had she ever told me this before? Yes, I said, she'd mentioned it a few times. She then began to rhapsodise about her sacred passage, at which point I feigned being late for something and hung up.

Not long after this phone call things in my house began to move, or were replaced by other things that were not my own. Small, innocuous things. For instance, in my office, where there had been a succulent on my desk, a pink stone paperweight took up residence; I couldn't find the jeans I wore regularly, and the dishes in the cupboard one day appeared almost entirely identical but a shade bluer. I asked my husband what had happened to the dishes and he claimed to have no idea what I was talking about, although, he said, you were fiddling around in the cupboard yesterday. On the fridge a recent picture of the both of us appeared to be taken from a slightly different angle.

One morning in the shower I came across bar of apricot-scented soap next to my husband's charcoal one. I went for a walk to clear my mind. It was bright morning, a week or so into the new year. The sun already causing licks of heat to distort the air above roofs and bitumen. I was finishing my walk, climbing up from our back garden which sloped into the gully—it's a steep path, and I stopped to take shade under a deflowered jacaranda—when I heard the unmistakable sound of my husband and me having sex.

I looked up through the kitchen window and saw a back, my back, pressing against the glass, one of my husband's hands gripped around my waist. I stood there sweating, watching them go at it—my husband thrusting enthusiastically—and experienced a strange hallucinatory dizziness as the heat went to my head.

I didn't storm in and stop them, scream bloody murder like I might have if it were another woman. I stood there entranced; they were beautiful to watch. The woman in the kitchen was, to her credit, much more flexible than me. One leg was bent beneath her so she was propped up on the table in a side kneel, while the other was lifted above my husband's shoulder, her chest turned towards the ceiling. Throughout the course of their fucking she did not seem to tire, nor did she stop mid-operation to reposition from a cramp. This, at the least, is why I cannot understand why my husband didn't know he was engaging in an extramarital activity.

After they finished, disappearing from the window, I walked in through the back door and poured myself a glass of water. I went in a haze to our bedroom, where my husband was lounging naked on the sheets, the window wide open, curtain billowing. He looked up at me with a lazy satisfied smile. His penis lay limp and wet. Why are you wearing clothes? he said. Come here. I went over to him and he took the glass out of my hand, pulled me onto the bed and asked if I wanted to go have lunch at that cafe we'd gone to the weekend before, what was it called? Through the window I saw, briefly, the mid-morning moon, almost full, like a worn-down coin, pale against the blue sky. I can only guess he believed I'd recently taken up yoga.

From then on, the things in my house were replaced with more frequency and audaciousness: my books, my underwear, the microwave. I sat down on the couch one evening, and although it looked precisely the same I knew I had never sat on that couch before. Good friends called and alluded to dinners or phone conversations I didn't remember having. I turned up to visit my mother one day and she looked confused, shook her head, the strips of grey at her temples twitching like whiskers, and said, but you came over yesterday.

And so on and on it went; my plants grew strange flowers, my bookshelf was alphabetised. I came into work one morning and my boss asked what the hell I was doing there. One evening, I was running late to my night class and ran a red light, and then from my car to the classroom. When I stopped to catch my breath outside the building, I saw, through the window, in my regular seat, I was already there, hunched over, scribbling in my notebook.

I went back to my car. The sky had darkened prematurely with heavy clouds, and as I drove, the heat broke in a large storm. I thought about the washing on the line, then began to cry. I'd become so sensitive; I cried over wet laundry. I found, as I continued to drive through the city I'd lived in my whole life, that I no longer recognised it. The tears dried up. I then remembered it was the date of the young man's exhibition and made a decisive left turn.

On entering the gallery I saw one of the sculptures he'd shown me on his phone; it was even larger than I thought, dazzling in the reflected light. On the wall there was a contextualising blurb. The work was called 'Self-portrait'. Below the blurb was a picture of the young man. I knew it was him, although the picture looked faded with age; it was his exact beard and green eyes, the slope of his nose and wide shoulders. He was holding a naked baby, both of them looking up at the camera. The caption read: 'My father and me, 1992.'

I turned around and left, then sat in the car for a long time, my head in my hands.

When I got home that evening, I unlocked the door to the feeling I'd already been home. I walked into the bedroom, where Anna stood folding laundry, rain hammering against the window.

Oh, she said, frowning, you're still here.

Yes, I said, it seems I am. There was a pause as we looked at each other like the first time we met, except neither of us smiled. Just let me get a few things, I said, and collected as much as I could, although in truth there was almost nothing of mine left in the house. I found a singlet, a bag, an ornamental incense holder, and left without saying goodbye to my husband.

I don't know precisely how much time passed from when I met Anna to when I left, although I remember the moon was almost full again, like it was the time I lay in bed in faux post-coital with my husband. I remember because I stopped in the middle of the night, after I'd driven from my old city to this new one, and looked up at the moon. I'd parked in front of a lake or large pond, which struck me as odd—a body of water residing so far up the Great Dividing Range. Shouldn't it, I thought, have over-flowed, spilled out to the landscape beneath?

The night sky had a fine layer of cloud and the moon emanated a glow like a halo, on the edges of which a rainbow circled. There was something wrong about the scene of the lake, the green bridge across it, the mountains cascading in the background. I sat in the car, the last of my belongings strewn across the back seat, trying to understand why I'd not driven south along the east coast to the next capital—a beachside city, more populace—but west, inwards. Something felt increasingly off-kilter. I wound down the window to let in the night breeze, but still couldn't shake the feeling, so sat there uneasy until the stress and exhaustion of the day took me to sleep.

It's only now that I understand what was wrong with the image: the moon, so bright in the sky, had no twin reflected in the black water. The surface remained obsidian—impenetrable.

I've taken up residence in a cheap hotel named after the English botanist who 'discovered' and subsequently colonised the city for its rich, fertile soil. He is responsible, I think, for the city's ongoing obsession with gardens. With planting, every year, flowers of foreign colours and temperament.

By day I walk the streets, wandering and wondering what has brought me here and what it is I am meant to do with myself. It took me a while to understand why the place gave me a feeling of deja vu, until one day, walking under the trees that infamously line the streets, I recognised their bright leaves and wide, intricate ridged bark—they were the same trees as the one in the front garden of Reilly's house. The one the young man had described to me. Elated with my recognition, I rushed back to the hotel to confirm it with the receptionist, but he only frowned at me over his glasses. He had a fantastic thinning head of hair, with two inches of fuzz that stood up defiantly; I could see directly through it to the hospital-green walls behind him. He was afraid, he said, I'd been gravely misinformed. Those trees, he said, were in fact introduced in 1822, by way of China. He knew this, he said, because they were introduced by the very man the hotel I was staying at was named after. The trees were still considered, the receptionist said, one of his greatest botanical discoveries. Although, he added conspiratorially, they'd existed in Asia for millennia. They were not, he was quick to inform me, naturalised. The trees remain an invasive species. Their roots, he said, removing his glasses and cleaning them with a small cloth, curl deep into the soil, greedy for sustenance; they are still a great threat to native species— eucalyptus and koalas, predominately. Native birds, too, tend to avoid them, he added. Despite this, he said, replacing his glasses, they are impossible to get rid of because many locals fear they would lose their livelihood if the council were to do so. I frowned, and he shrugged, and said, tourism. Perhaps, he said sympathetically, I was mistaken.

I returned to my room upstairs and drew the curtain open. A frenzy of lorikeets emanated from two of the trees below. Although their screeching drowned out ambient street nose, among the dense leaves, I couldn't spot a single bird. The sun set the city in orange.

Walking each day, it's hard to ignore that the streets are extremely wide, even in the city centre—as wide as they would've been when horses pulled carriages though them. Each day, increasingly, I understand the city as existing as a veneer. Its insistence on foreign beauty in its various museums, mementos, statues—not on the native land and people, but to the accomplishments of the settlers, of train lines built and places conquered—as an ongoing ode to colonisation.

Perhaps all this is why the place has an eerie ambiance, nothing is as it should be, and, therefore, it feels as if anything could happen—like snow might start falling mid-summer. As if the plants craved the temperament of their homeland and filled the city with longing.

I am in constant grief, as if a piece of this place has broken off and become lodged in my throat. I cannot concentrate, and the summer, now almost always in a state of humidity on the cusp of rain has made me constantly wet.

I'm not sure how long I can sustain this state of mourning. I don't believe I want to stay here but something is preventing me from leaving. It's not a place where I feel at ease, but I can't deny it's a very friendly town. Since coming here, strangers have stopped to ask me how I am. They wave from their cars. The shop attendant calls me darling, and tells me about his son's football game, says not to come too close, his breath is terrible, he's getting an abscess removed later that day.

Just last week, I was walking though one of the gardens, the flowers long dead, when a woman wheeling a pram and wearing a complicated head wrap called out to me. Anne! she said, and although this is not quite my name I turned around. Maryanne! She came as quickly as she could over the pebbled path. How *are* you? she said, almost yelling over her screaming toddler.

Is he alright? I asked, peering into the pram.

Oh, never mind him. Yesterday, she said, an edge to her voice, he began to cry—and here two streams of water tracked down her own face—because, she sniffed, he didn't like the texture of tomatoes. But, anyway, the woman rocked the pram back and forth, wiped the tears off her face, we're getting a sitter for our house-warming. I've been meaning to get in contact with you. Day after tomorrow. Here, she said, and pulled out a piece of paper and pen on which she scribbled down details, thrust it onto me, and, with a harassed-looking wave, shot off again.

As I climbed up the stairs to the stranger's apartment, the most unusual feeling came over me. I began to feel as if I'd walked this way before. As if, despite knowing I hadn't met anyone at the party, I was about to catch up with old friends. When I rang the doorbell a man I'd never seen before answered it, but I knew already, as I looked at him, the smell of his neck, the taste of him.

An odd lightness overcame me, like I was finally adjusting to the altitude of the place. I felt, as I rubbed my thumb over my fingertips, as if their prints would dissolve.

Times You Let Anger
Slip Out Your Throat

What have you done? You've let it slip, fall, again. Feel: nothing but the ridged tendons of your arms. See: the blur of streetlights, empty packet of Cheetos animated in wind, spinning down the road. What have you done? Sweet summer, five am, tank top sticking to your stomach, hoodie on, hood down, unzipped, sleeves rolled up, hardly needed. Your Docs make sweet slicking noises as your peel them off the pavement: *thit thit*. Smell: vodka cranberries, regurgitated, a joint snuck into the smoker's section, bleach from your mop bucket. Any dew that might have beaded on the grass has long since evaporated in the heat of the night. If you were of sound mind, head, thinking, feeling; if you were to notice how your fingers are burning, red, fist-clenched; if you realised your head humming with more than shots of Jameson behind the bar, that words have crept into your brain to niggle on your walk home, where you can't listen to music, a podcast, can't even hum to yourself, because you are a woman walking home alone at night, where all you can do is march onward, turn down Smith Street, in these minutes before sunrise, looking behind you, letting the words rattle inside your head.

Jessie,   the shifts when I need
could you clean   the girls
asked me how I was, then turned   ignored me
just catch an uber home, Jesus,
know how she is with vomit   heard from you in
of your pay   bottle opener?
happened to you
joking, I'm joking   woooeee   much is a jug of
the fuck have you

If you had noticed all of this—if you were in tune with your body, not focused on the bright lights approaching, red lights receding, rustles, creaks, a car alarm suddenly going off— you would know your anger has slipped out of your throat, animated your body. Instead you are buzzing with the indignity of walking home alone at night, again, after nine hours of dealing with drunks, down to the share house with crusted dishes overloading the sink, with piss on the bathroom floor, the same half-drunk bottle of Melbourne Bitter on the edge of the bath, newspaper over the crack in your bedroom window, dead mice in the walls, parties next door cackling well into the dawn. How glamorously you're living! No social life. Plenty of excuses for someone to stop loving you—all for the privilege of twenty dollars an hour, five dollars under minimum. But you know, you're lucky you're not on sixteen. You are walking home down Smith Street, nails cutting into your palm. You are shaking; you are not cold. Turn left here, down the brightest road that will take you to Brunswick Street, down Brunswick for a while, then a few streets to home.

Stop: a man is walking towards you from the other end of the street. He doesn't cross the way some men do, to let you know they mean no harm, the way other men do to make you think they mean no harm.

sweethe

Oh it's like
wouldn't   *where the 86 tram*
          you alone   *completely high*
               anyway

alright?

ve got some change

Breathe: he's got a dog with him. One of those rust-coloured poodle-crosses that do not belong—although you're against making generalisations—to night-roaming rapists. He's wearing a navy North Face jacket. Relax: just a yuppie walking his dog at the crack of dawn.

Relax? How, when your shins are burning. When you're breathing in quick, shallow breaths. It has slipped from your throat, warmed up your body, filled the whole street. When the man is about to pass you, he crosses the road, looks at you like you're the danger.

The morning hums, cars passing in the street behind you, your own footsteps, your breathing, *thit, thit, thuuu, huuuhh.* It's here when you're alone with your own rhythm that you understand the buzz in your head. You know what it is. You are angry, radiating, glowing, fucking vibrating with anger, but awareness is not a cure. More like recognising an old friend you didn't want to run into.

You are: six, new school, swinging from the monkey bars. You have made a friend, wonky pigtails, dirty face. The both of you are busy on a quest. You are: explorers on a fairy island, where the fairy queen—the mermaid fairy queen—owns a pet chinchilla. You must save the queen's chinchilla. Your imagination is standard for a six-year-old, but you are having fun. A boy with pale eyes comes over.

ugly

says girls aren't

your dad poor

why don't   *have a*

You are on the ground on top of him. You have his thin hair between your fingers, pulling him down to the sandpit. It is clear, from the look on his face, that this is not what happens when he bullies other kids. You grab a fistful of sand, pummel your feet into his body, wrestling, your face red, shiny from screaming, until an adult pulls you off.

Here on the street you know you are angry because you've been here so many times before. Your eyesight is blurry with tears that well, overflow, slip down your cheek. You are aware of what is happening at this point, the alcohol is wearing off, but that doesn't make it go away.

You are: twelve. A new enemy: a boy who won't leave you alone. You have told him to stop, stop handing you notes, bringing you roses he's pulled roughly from his neighbour's garden, showing you the cuts from the thorns as proof of his love. The teachers have asked you to be kind.

> *special, dear*
> *know what he's doing. Going   love*
> *not really hurt   doesn't*
> *you love*
>
> *just ignore*
>
> *it'll go*

But each morning when he comes to single you out, you can't ignore him. Tears bead, fall down your face. You do not know that tears mean you're upset. You know if you could laugh at him, like the other kids do, maybe he would leave you alone. But: he doesn't do these things to the other kids. Also: you can't laugh, you don't want to be cruel, you just want him to stop. You don't know that what he is making you feel is upset because you turn everything into anger. One morning when he comes to you, you run away, but he follows. He just wanted to sing you a song. It's 'Push Up' by the Freestylers, charting at number two in this year, 2004. You scream, hit, hit, hit, but not at him, your fists against the wall, your head slamming up against the brick. This is how they find you, flinging yourself at the wall, screaming, lit up in red. When they call your father in, the boy is not mentioned.

too old   push up
that your daughter has   your body

                                                        display

        her mother?   our position to   next   to mine
        know what goes on at   behavioural issues
    not really

Turn right onto Brunswick Street. You know what is happening
to your body, you've felt this before. There are still people about
here, it's Saturday night/Sunday morning. Three women, skinny
jeans, tight ponytails, cling to one another outside a 7Eleven.

                                                    No I love

                        just so lucky

        god we're so   metallic taste

                                                where's Justin

            stale

You stand at the pedestrian crossing. It throbs up again. *Fuck*, you
scream; it slips out your throat before you can catch it. A man
with a Deliveroo bag glances at you, takes a step back. Across the
street a bouncer lifts a radio to his mouth, but most everyone else
is too drunk, making too much noise, to care. The trio of women
start to giggle. One of them has been crying too: the glitter from
her eye makeup has rippled down her face, illuminating collarbones, cheeks, nose tip. The little red man still flashes but you
cross the street anyway. You beat the palm of your hand against
your temple, *thump, thump, thump,* like you can knock it free.
But it's too late, it's slipped out, you are moving through it. You
need to be home.

You are: fourteen, new school, a boy who looks just like your primary school bully. Why do they all look the same? Vacant eyes, some rotund red father they imitate for love. He is bigger than you, stupider than you, lacks imagination. He thinks it's hilarious to tell girls to go make a sandwich.

This year is the year of the breasts. The year of the tits— he calls them tits. He will draw them, every type, small, big, dangling, perky, areolae as big as apples. He will grab whichever ones come his way. At lunchtime, at the bell rush, he says, Nice tits, Jess. Without pausing to think, without breaking stride, you walk over to him, drive your foot into his groin. When he falls, you slam your fist into his nose. You are breathing heavily, *thuuu, uuun,* but it was a slick, quick anger that spilled out then left.

frankly,

she's not suspended

want anything   *don't expect*

no

You know what it looks like, what it feels like, because in truth it feels like everything. You are not good at in-between emotions; you have witnessed, through your lifetime, yourself whittle out the nuance of frustration, upset, disappointment. You have transformed it, all of it through your body, into something that rattles then explodes.

You know what is happening because you have been here before. But you thought you had a handle on it, didn't you, thought you had learnt to untangle your anger. You know, too, what you are meant to do to stop it. Count backwards from ten. Breathe.

In through your nose.

Out through your mouth.

TEN

Nostrils flare, inhale.

You are turning off Brunswick Street now. No streetlights. No people either. Silence, almost, occasional waft of noise from the main road. Out through your mouth.

NINE

You thought you had a handle on it. In through your nose. The sun is rising, the birds have begun to wake in sweet trills. But you're walking faster still—what is that?

EIGHT

Up there, a person, a woman, like you walking home alone at night—in the early morning. Out through your mouth.

SEVEN

But why are you walking faster, why are your hands still burning, clenched, why are tears still streaming down your cheeks?

SIX

Out through your mouth. But you remember, don't you, the last time this happened. It wasn't due to a boy teasing you, it wasn't *teenage hormones,* it wasn't a man who wanted to take something from you. It was when you were happy, living in another city, drunk on gin, out with friends. A woman you were with, a woman you liked, looked down at you, or you thought she did. You—

FIVE

—what happened? You were having a nice night. A liquid clear happy night. You had another drink when you should have gone home. What happened? The way she looked at you—what was it? You flung your glass down right there—shattering it. *Who the fuck did she think she was? Fucking—*

FOUR

Yes, you remember what happened the last time you did this, don't you? They way your friends reacted. *We.   didn't realise Such bad   Anger issue*

No fucking shit. Took them that long to realise they didn't want to be around you. The last time you did this, you did this to a woman. Now here you are, a woman walking down the street, two women, one behind the other. She has not noticed you yet. But you do not look like this woman, who has long hair, a dress, stockings, sensible heels. You do not look womanly, do you? Because you have to walk home alone at night most nights. Because you got too angry being treated like a woman. This is why you wear your hair in a buzzcut. Why you lift weights before work, jaw clenched, counting backwards from ten, breathe in, breathe out. Why you wear a sports bra, your breasts strapped into pectorals. In silhouette, you are not a woman, walking home behind another woman walking home. You are someone who is following a woman home. Your fists balled up, anger radiating out of you to the street. The sun has risen now. The last time this happened, it was you screaming at another woman, *Fucking condescending bitch.*

THREE

Why couldn't you be like her, this woman in front of you, all soft, lovely, all sweet silhouette, no deep premature wrinkles in her forehead, you bet, she has a nice life, you bet. What life did you have to lead, *what did you have to do*, oh no, this has slipped out your tongue too, you monster. Slipped out? You screamed it, don't you have any control? What's wrong with you? She looks behind her, alarmed, what have you done? Now you are running, screaming, *What did you have to do?* She looks again behind her before she starts running too, clutching her handbag to her side. This time when she looks, you catch the angle of her face. You think, No, it can't be, but now, the both of you running, you see better the curve of her back, hair the same shade as yours, deja vu. Think: of course, this is you—you without anger.

TWO

Just as you are about to reach her, you see her face again, but— she is not you, just has similar features. Widow's peak, large eyes, mole on her neck. You falter. The sun is climbing, she is screaming, running as fast as she can, you are right behind her. This is not a metaphor. She is not you. You are chasing a woman down the street. She sees you too, sees you are a woman. For a second her fear snaps to confusion. Just as your arms reach out to meet her, miraculously a side street is there, you turn down it, taking your burning body away, away from her, as fast as you can, one foot after another. Face tight from the salt of your tears. Run, run, run. You do not know where you are going. Stop in a park, fall to your knees, close your eyes, chest aching. Swift sobs break out your nose, your mouth. What have you done? Let your anger slip out your throat, for what? Did you want that woman to be terrified, see the burning light, right before you—no.

ONE

You raise your face to the sky, but through the film of your eyelids, all you see is red.

Two Hundred and One Days
of Forests Burning

I have become one of those women who talk with their hands, despite my ever-present effort to be a woman who talks with her words and purposeful silences, hands still at my sides, perhaps raising a glass—coffee, water, dirty martini—to my lips. But here I am brandishing my digits at you like I'm trying to conjure the dead. Please don't ask me how this happened. I don't know, I don't want to talk about it. It's got even worse recently. I've started flapping my hands at inanimate objects—furniture, walls, kitchen appliances. Yesterday, when I got into a disagreement with the fridge about the ice, I ended up flapping and flailing like a startled pigeon.

In my defence, the fridge was genuinely infuriating. She has stopped giving me ice. Not ice *cubes*, anyway. She gives me ice *shards*. The kind typically covered in bright syrup and sold at fetes to sticky children and their nostalgic parents.

A slushie, is what it is. The fridge now gives me slushies.

I can see in hindsight it was unfair, my reaction—out of context, it does not look good. I didn't say I was proud. But understand, this is about the fourth time recently I've gone to the refrigerator in the morning, and instead of the satisfying *plonk plonk plonk* of my perfectly cubed ice splashing into the water, I've experienced the *whir* and *plop*. *Whir* as the fridge grinds the ice into a mush and then *plop* as it fills my glass to brimming with a glorified slop. As the glass is already half filled, the water gushes out like a geyser and soaks me—a sensation not unlike being pricked with a thousand needles.

On a good day, I remind myself that the fridge has feelings. That it is not okay to lash out at the fridge just because. On a good day I ask the fridge if it wouldn't mind recalibrating its ice-giving method so I can have my usual three, large, intact ice cubes. I do this in a calm, soothing voice. I do not tell it to make the ice the way it *knows* I like my ice. The way it *normally* makes the ice. The way it has been making it going on eight months now. No, I ask nicely. This is only, of course, after I've already asked koKo to clean up the spillage, please, and got another half full glass of water. Half full: look at me, the optimist. I ask nicely because of all our appliances the fridge is particularly sensitive. I forgot to say good morning once and she froze my cauliflower. God, why am I telling you this?

Yesterday was not a good day. First I shrieked at the rude awakening. One second sleepily trying to hydrate, the next fully conscious and saturated, my nipples threatening to shred my nightgown into rags. Then I directed my shrieking *at* the fridge, screaming how on God's Green Earth could something so supposedly sophisticated be so incompetent, and just what the fuck did I have to do to get my three cubes of ice in the morning, please? All the while, mind you, my hands are working like over-active antennae. So I'm standing there flapping like an idiot, and the fridge—Jesus—the fridge responds that *my husband* prefers the slushie water and has asked specifically, just that morning, to ensure that ice shards are made and not ice cubes. So I said, Well I'm not my husband and you know I'm not my husband and I know you know I'm not my fucking husband, so please, for the love of god, I will ask you the next time I want to freeze my tits off this early in the am. Christ, I sound like my mother. I know, I know, I'm getting nitpicky, but I'm getting to the point, I promise.

The fridge tried to explain to me the differences in temperature required for my ice preferences and my husband's, her voice rising to this horrible noise not unlike crows having a go at a chalk-board. I know I really should have stopped there. But I didn't. Instead I said, Well, I want to be able to have ice cubes whenever I want; I think you're overestimating how much I care about how perfect my ice cubes are, just any old ice cubes would do. And, for that matter, why exactly did my husband's ice preferences super-sede my own, considering we'd bought her together, when I had a job, and owned her, therefore, together, equally.

That was where I really crossed a line. Although the fridge is prone to crying, generally speaking you can calm her down if you apologise enough, if you assure her that she is a wonderful fridge and you appreciate how hard she works and you don't want her to feel like she's being taken for granted. But the fridge does not like to be reminded that she is property, that she is our posses-sion. It upsets her. It would upset anyone, I suppose. I guess I lost my temper. She is yet to speak to me.

I used to do that a lot—lose my temper. I wonder if you've forgiven me, I'm not so sure you should. I know what you'd say about this, that I seem to care more about the feelings of inanimate objects than the state of—I know what you would say. You could be right, because the worst thing through all this, as I was yelling at the fridge, and apparently conducting an invisible orchestra meanwhile, is that koKo was in the hallway cowering at all the noise. I don't like to be like that in front of koKo. Although—I know what you would say about him too. I'm not an idiot. I read your book of poetry, I should say, I guess that's why I'm calling, even though I can't stop with this fridge bullshit. I'm getting to it, please just—I'm getting to it.

I turned away from the fridge, telling her that tomorrow she would make me three regular goddamn ice cubes—which she hasn't, mind you—and I would be talking about this to my husband when he got back from whatever 'work trip' he was currently balls-deep in, just watch me. And when I turned around, koKo was there.

I tried to call him to me but when I stepped towards him he spooked and ran off. It took me a whole half-hour to get him off the top of the cupboard and when I did he was still shaking, but I wrapped him in a towel and shushed and held him until eventually he began to make his napping noises, this soft chirping—like a cat imitating a bird. I dozed off with him on the couch and we must have been there a while, because when I woke to a gradual dimming—smog moving over the sun, miraculous that it was out at all—my nightgown was dry and the fridge was no longer crying. It wasn't smog, though, but a link he'd sent me, prepaid, for your book of poetry, which had opened on the wall, shadowing over us. He likes to remind me, I think, about the decision I made.

The water has been changing colour again, have you noticed? I suppose you have. The lake that turned pink. Smell's unbelievable. I went to see it, on one of my days off a few months ago, although I suppose all my days are off now. Salt, they said at first. It really did used to happen, water turning pink from salt, so I guess everyone thought it was fine, a good sign even. That something was going back to normal. But now, with the reserve north of the city gone orange, and the other river too—I say the other river because the river near our house has turned this off greeny-blue. Not river-green, or sea-blue, an odd colour, like it's from another world. I've been walking down there every day to see if it's changed. Become a shade lighter or deeper, more nuclear. It's hard to say which—of course you've heard all this, although I don't think it makes the news anymore. Hard to be noteworthy, I suppose, when the world is on fire. Two hundred days, according to your collection. How accurate is it? I know I could look this up but I've decided not to. To try not to anymore. When the news comes on in the morning I tell him to shut up. So, huh, maybe they do still report on the river, I wouldn't know. I only mention it because it sounds poetic—the coloured water. You would tell me off for this. Low-hanging fruit.

The poems are very good, I'm sure you know. Or some days you know, and other days you think they're awful. Maybe you don't think of them at all. I read them all in one go, yesterday right here in the living room. I've not decided if I forgive you just yet, so I don't know why I'm recording. At first I read on the couch, then I stood and stretched, pages moving to whatever surface

I was looking at, shadows shifting. I don't know how it started but whenever I stretch, usually in the morning to stop myself from becoming like this—all hands and words and mania—koKo starts to mimic me. He stands next to me and stretches. My arms and his limbs in the air as we lean into a squat, downward dog changing to lion pose, his little round head rotating to calculate my next move. Yesterday, he copied me the entire time. It's cute in a way, this weird mirroring. You would find it creepy, I'm sure.

Stretching helps with the dizziness, I don't know how. From up here, looking down at the bottom of the building—and you know how I am with heights—I feel more in control of my body. It's funny, while I've been saying this, spinning my arms around, koKo has been standing behind me; I've just caught sight of his reflection. He's standing behind me waving his arms around, copying me. I wonder how long he's been there. The whole time? You're probably the only one who'll know—I've been prattling on, I don't think I can watch it back. I might just end up sending the whole thing.

I was surprised how much I was in the book. To an outsider it wouldn't be obvious, but I can tell when you've stolen my movements, the way I drink my coffee in the morning, complain about work. I thought I wouldn't be in it at all considering you're a *political* poet. But there I was, you falling out of love with me. Is that really how it went; is that what you think of me? You always were a good editor.

I've kept up the stretching, even though the dizziness doesn't matter so much anymore with the fog. Smog. Sometimes, when it's clear up here but the ground is obscured with a thick grey layer like a dirty blanket, it feels like the building is rising out of nowhere into a sort of heaven. It weirdly helps in a way; it feels like floating, like there's no reference point to be dizzy from.

Ah, I see koKo has moved on. He got bored I suppose, now that I've stopped swatting around like I'm walking through a cloud of gnats. I'm feeling a little calmer now, more like myself. I would have preferred to start like this, but I'm not sure I would have begun at all if I'd been calm—and I don't think I can again.

After I read your book, I went for one of my walks to the river. Out there it's so—it feels like the air has compressed itself, like it's trying to squeeze your body into a smaller space, like your lungs are fighting to stay inflated. The density makes you sweat immediately and it's hard work getting to the river. It's not just the breathing, it's like moving through something other than air. I like it in a way. I think that's why I do all this, why I do yoga and throw my hands around, because as much as I want to be composed, to be articulate with words alone, a lot of the time it's like I need to physically move something out of me. Like I need to feel something bodily in order to be free of it.

Not all of us can be like you, please understand.

It was an unusually nice day on my walk yesterday. Despite the anniversary. There was no one out on the street, and the sun was coming through the clouds. That's how nice a day it was— you could mistake the smog for clouds.

I went to this crossing I like on the river. It's quite a walk away, but I like a particular pedestrian bridge where you can stand on the top of the arch. From there you can pretend that the city isn't right behind you, and if you go at the right time of day, as the sun begins to set, which I did yesterday, the river looks almost a normal colour.

The weird thing about all this is the birds seem fine. I'm sure they're not. I'm sure if you took a scalpel to them they'd be full of bright-coloured plastic, poking into their organs, stuck at sharp angles in their necks. That a reading of their bloodwork would be riddled with toxic chemicals. That their eyesight would be awful, their feather oil horribly and irredeemably wrong. But it isn't my job to worry about that kind of stuff anymore. And yesterday down at the river the birds, as I say, seemed fine. There were a lot of them, pigeons, seagulls, ducks—shovelers, pink-eared, wood—a family of black swans, even a pair of little black cormorants drying their wings on the water's edge. All these different birds swimming around, not quibbling or squawking at one another, standing on rocks cleaning their feathers, one or two divers licking into the water, reappearing a few feet away. I was standing there looking at them and, for just a moment, I felt calm. It occurs to me now that those probably weren't real birds, that they have, like our appliances, been replaced with something more reassuring, and of course I didn't have the right to feel calm, standing there ignoring the world blazing around me. But I haven't felt calm for months, I've been stretching and walking and flailing and just trying to not feel like *that* all the time. Although what does it matter at this rate, if someone like me isn't calm? I know what you would say about this, about my duty as a democratic citizen, about my ability to ignore being a part of my privilege; don't think I'm so daft, don't think I don't know that it was meant to be you with this life, and me with yours, don't think I don't know. I got exhausted, understand, it's fine for someone like you to decide to be good, but I got so exhausted—my life was always exhausting, from the very beginning, not like yours. And it just felt like, for once, I could choose to be someone else, something else, it's so easy to be a possession. And ah. Not all of us can be as good as you. I think maybe you know this. That's what's really fucking annoying: that you'd understand. That maybe you even think that you're not good, Eloise. That it is an impossible thing to be good at a time like this, but you are.

Jesus.

On the bridge yesterday when I felt calm the strangest thing happened. The birds, not all at once, but little by little, they all turned and drifted toward me. It was the strangest thing. All these birds started at me from different crevasses along the river bank, behind me even. Black swans nipping worms out of the grass perked up, ibis drifted in from the rocks, a mallard that was already swimming about-faced. And all of them kept on toward this point—toward me—and eventually they looked as if they were going to collide, right below my line of sight. It looked like they were going to crash, but—and then they didn't. All at once the sun, cresting the horizon, threw peach colours over the sky, and the peaks of the blue-green ripples highlighted with pinks and orange in the tail of its refection. And the birds— right when this was happening—the birds, they just passed one another, just passed by. And for a moment, from above, right as they were passing through, it looked like a busy intersection, all this colour and birds weaving together.

And then the smog moved back over the sun, and the birds kept on swimming in the direction they were going. After a few seconds, it didn't even look like they'd congregated in the one spot like that, and the water had gone off again, this opaque green-blue. Everything just went back to normal. It was the strangest thing.

Not all of us can be as good as you, even if we try. What's so upsetting is that of all things, it's the fridge that reassures me— when I feel that I've given up on a better life, a more responsible life, it's the fridge that reminds me that there's only so much one person can do, that I can't possibly be expected to take on every crisis, that of course it's understandable that I chose the easier route and why don't I sit down and she'll make me a strawberry milk. And now not even she will talk to me. Not that I ever believed her. I think it's more that some of us aren't destined to be good. That we can't be good, even if we try. Or maybe it's that we don't know how to try. We've forgotten. I think that's why I'm calling—I've forgotten how to be good.

When the River Floods Our House

Okay, sure, we would like to think we'd do
better. Given the opportunity. Given the
opportunity between doing the right thing
(laugh it off, be secure in our relationship)
and the wrong thing (accuse our husbands,
wives, partners, lovers of all sorts of deviant
behaviour) we would like to think we'd chose
the former. We would like to think we could
handle our particular neuroses on our own,
deal with any issues we may have as they
arise, in a calm and insightful manner.
That we could pour two glasses of
wine, cook a nice meal—charred
greens, beetroot glaze, potatoes,
rosemary—cuddle on the couch to
watch one of those three-hour sagas

directed by Unpronounceable
Russian Man Number Two, and
simply bring up the matter, talk it
through. Perhaps when we're making
popcorn, or trying to remember the
log-in to whatever esoteric streaming service
they subscribe to. Us: Hey, I noticed Valerie's
been giving you a lot of attention lately. Is it
underscore or dash? Them: Yeah, I know, it's a
little annoying really. Us: Not anything I have to
worry about, is it? Them: Don't be ridiculous, I love
you. Underscore. Or alternatively. Them: [passionate kiss,
reaching behind you to steal popcorn] Valerie who? Or
alternatively, alternatively [passionate kiss, hands pulling
down pants] This movie *is* boring, isn't it? We like to think
we are pragmatic people, we really do. That if something
starts to bother us, to percolate, to metabolise our
communication skills, we will get a therapist. Go for
long walks. Do yoga. Start kickboxing. Take control
of our own lives. We like to think of ourselves as
good people. Especially when we have certain
things going for us in life—the type of house
we grew up in, the colour of our skin, the
educational institution we graduated from—
which is to say we are in a much better
position than most to do things like take
control of our lives. We would like to
think, given our privileges, that we have
the self-awareness to not take out our

issues on other people. That we are not in danger
of becoming a passive-aggressive, or just regularly
aggressive, person. People who put down the
wineglass a little harder than necessary, who sigh
loudly as they do the dishes, who let their
entrances and exits be known. Who declare, every
time there is a gas or electricity or water bill, that
of course this expense had to come right *now*, at this
time; of all the times it possibly could have come, it
came just now, at this moment in our lives, just
especially to make whatever personal melodrama we are
currently enacting, worse. Even though water and gas
and electricity bills are, in fact, prone to coming at very
predictable time brackets, every quarter. We would like
to think instead that we can be the person who finally
organises the cupboard. What super account do we
have anyway? Yes, we will change to that ethical
bank. Yes, we can concede, we liked the movie, it
was just the idea of sitting down and watching
a long black and white film that we did not
enjoy, not the actual experience of it. We had
a mental block around it, so to speak. We
want to be the person who can admit
they are wrong. Who, when
the leak in the basement is
getting noticeably worse,
calls a plumber, and
not the kind who
simply places another

receptacle under the drip.
We would like to think we
are the person who,
when we see that
Valerie is,
once again,
flirting
with
our
husband,
would simply look
at our husband,
who is aware of this behaviour,
and is aware, what's more, that
this behaviour bothers us, and
wink at him, throw him a
winning smile. We would like
to be able to let things go,
just once. But as it stands,
sometimes we are the person on
our third, leaning against the
kitchen counter of our very dear
friend, listening to our very dear
friend complain about their boss, who
really does sound like an arsehole, and
using every ounce of our effort to not
mock Valerie behind her back. Valerie, in
the living room, slapping our husband's arm,
being shrill: Stop it, Mark! You're being mean

to me! Mark's being mean to me!
(Mark is not being mean to her; she
does not want Mark to Stop It.) As it
stands, it sounds like a lot of paperwork. As
it stands, the basement is full of pot plants,
slowly watering. As it stands, we use words like
'shrill' to describe other women when we know
perfectly well how disgusting and misogynistic it is
to do so. As it stands, a large storm is coming, on
various phone screens around the party, in the digital
ether it flows from the northwest, red at its centre,
bleeding into orange, yellow, growing into a green and blue
tail as it comes towards and then engulfs Brisbane,
disappears, ebbs to starts the pixel dance again. There is a
storm coming, and once it starts raining it will not stop for
two weeks. We would like to think we are the person who,
when things like rain and utility bills and flirtatious
acquaintances come and, in our eyes, try to disrupt our
Nice Slice Of Life we have Worked Hard To Build,
would take it on the chin. Think of the bigger
picture. How does it really matter, in the scheme
of things, when the heatwaves are getting longer,
and the infamous Brisbane storms are getting
more and more violent? When the entire
north of the country is getting very
uninhabitable, very, very quickly, and it is
difficult to function throughout the
summer months unless you are insulated
with air-conditioners and a certain

socio-economic status? We
would like to think, when
the Going Gets Tough, that
we could invoke God, or
gods, or whatever
omnipresence we believe in,
to help us through this one
tough bit, get us through to the
other side, because we know that
this thing will not matter, not really,
in the long run. We know that there *is*
an 'other' side. We hope that, if we
happen to not be religious, we can find
solace in good people, the natural world,
and the animals that occupy it. That we
are able to find meaning and purpose
in Doing The Right Thing,
whatever that means. Perhaps we
feel very connected to a specific
beach, or life guru, or pink
crystals. Whatever works,
we try not to judge.
Perhaps we remember,
as a child, going to
Canada with our
father and his new
girlfriend to visit
her family on a
farm in the north

of Winnipeg. Perhaps we
remember one night, playing
sardines in a can with her horde of
young cousins and nieces and nephews,
and the feeling of unity and fun that
only-children do not generally get to
experience. Only-children with truant
mothers, and stepmothers who are not interested
in subverting certain tropes or clichés regarding
stepmotherhood—who are keen to stick to genre, so
to speak. Perhaps we remember being on top of an old
windmill, lying sardined amongst the other children,
while another counted to one hundred somewhere below.
Perhaps we remember then, the sky splitting in some
luminescent green ribbon, and the loud gasp we let out
as it snaked its way across the black sky. Perhaps we
sat up and totally bungled our hiding spot for
everyone, and the other children found us, in our
antipodean awe of the lights, funny, when it was
to them nothing special, and certainly not a
good reason to forfeit such an ingenious
hiding spot. Perhaps we remember how
we felt: in community, loved, as if the sky
had opened up and told us life is
beautiful, anything is possible, or
something completely trite that
only someone seeing the northern
lights for the first time would ever
think—something we would never

admit we one hundred percent
agree with. And, although we may
not worship any deity, we have,
nevertheless, known that we only
ever want to make other people feel as we
did in that moment.   But sometimes
we forget. Sometimes, all we can think about is
the chafing that's developed from overwearing our
only pair of linen pants. Sometimes, the storm is worse
than predicted, and sends everybody home early,
and we do not say goodbye to Valerie, or even
acknowledge her existence as we leave the party, even
though we know she will be hurt by this behaviour,
because it becomes easier, once you know someone, to be
cruel. To curate your cruelness. Sometimes, we call an old
friend an acquaintance when they make a habit of
flirting with our husbands. The storm has grown red and
angrier on the phone screen, but outside the car the sky
is a deep plum-purple, lightning cracking through the
clouds. Sometimes, we pretend not to hear our
husbands, over the rain that is starting to
ding rather than splatter, when he asks
if we are okay. Sometimes we just close
our eyes and lean our head back, even
when he's volunteered to be the
designated driver, again, and is now
driving in rain so heavy he can do
nothing more than trust the
white line. Even when he is the

type of man who would
never do something so
horrendously clichéd as
sleep with a younger,
prettier woman. He is, we
know, a true avant-gardist.
We would like to think we are well
adjusted. That we are not in danger of
becoming one of those women with the
haircut, asking for the manager. That we can
regulate our responses, because we are in a
position to do so. Because we should know better.
Because we know that developing certain attitudes
towards certain people because they continue to
flirt with our husbands is really our own little
problem we'll just have to learn to deal with. And
what is it, really, to flirt? Harmless. Better, a form
of communication. A way to let people know
they are desired, and we all like to be desired, don't
we? (And we are guilty, ourselves, of flirting,
aren't we?) And we know even as we are
running from the car to the house,
soaked from the five-second
sprint, that there are always other
dynamics at play. We know this
because we are highly educated
women, with masters or PhDs
in women's studies or
communication, or

psychology, or social work, et al. At
the very least we are modern women,
we have bachelor's degrees or access to
articles and think-pieces on which to
further educate ourselves. We have read the
literature, and we know there are always other
things to consider. We know that certain
feelings towards other women serve only the
purpose of spreading discord, and that it has
historically been very convenient for the type of
people that tend to make women feel this way towards
each other (men) if women are suspicious and mean to
each other, instead of kind and community building. We
know, furthermore, that when we are callous and cruel
towards women who belong to minorities we do not
belong to there are always other things to consider.
Histories, implications. Hierarchies we are perpetuating
instead of tearing down. That there is not a little bit
of condescension involved in being unable to have an
open and honest conversation with Valerie about
our grievances. We know, that is to say,
jealousy is a patriarchal structure, and
we don't like sticking to structure. But
it's hard to stop a story we've read so
many times before. To reinvent the
genre. To swim out of the current.
It is hard sometimes to decide to
go and check on the drip in the
basement when it is raining,

when we know it will be worse. It is hard to keep our cool when,
on entering
       the basement,
              we realise
                    the
                       pipe
                           dripping
                     is
                    the
                    least
                    of
                    our
                    worries. That the river
our house backs onto has swollen so quickly it has flooded the
basement, the basement is now in the river, and so is our washing
machine and a basket of laundry, clothes bobbing like disintegrating toffee apples. We want to be the person who laughs and
tries to save the drowned plants, and thinks not of the broken
washing machine, but about the variety of fungi that will bloom
in the garden once the river has receded. Who does not completely
fucking lose it right there, in our basement, shin-deep in brown
river water. Who answers our father's calls all the time, and not
just when it is convenient to do so. Who says hello and reassures him we are okay, there's just a bit of water in the basement,
who does not derail the conversation to ask if he remembers
the northern lights. The way they had filled the sky with greenness, how we'd been expecting all kinds of colours, the blues and
purples and pinks we know the lights to look like. The way we
found its overwhelming greenness, if anything, more magnetic.

Who, when he says there weren't any northern lights that night—what on earth are we talking about, they were predicted to show that night but it ended up being overcast, remember, we'd missed them—moves on with the more pressing issue at hand. Who does not stand there, in silence, looking at the intricate undulating patterns of the pipe water dripping into and getting carried away in the larger body of the river water. The person who does not hang up on our father when he says, What the hell are you doing, get out of the river water. And maybe we can be.

We can see a pale moth, fluttering, stuck between the frosted panes of the laundry window, its wings dusting the glass. We can wade over, reach up to the latch, and let it free. We can get out of the water.

As the Nation Still Mourns

January 10

It would be easy for me to say that when I took the job I didn't know. That I was hoodwinked, tricked. That the woman who employed me seemed, on paper, sensible—sensitive. That the job advertisement—ECOLOGIST WANTED—seemed serious at the time. It would be easy for me to say this. The media will no doubt use the picture of me taken two years ago on Fraser Island, hair tucked into my green parker, wide smile, turtle hatchling cupped in my hands—Caitlin Belgrave: researcher, environmentalist, sometimes amateur underwater photographer. Caitlin Belgrave, whose skills were appropriated for the entitled affluent. Or maybe I will be portrayed as a daft blonde—this is how my peers will see me, I know. People are happy to deny you agency when you look like me.

This is without thinking about those who knew my father, those who know I am my father's daughter, what they would say.

He and I don't have the same last name—intentionally on his part—to protect my privacy. Because that is all he ever wanted, to protect things. But imagine the headlines: *Reuben Greenfield's daughter tarnishes father's legacy, as the nation still mourns.*

My colleagues, my contemporaries, old university friends, will scroll through the article and say, *Caity, Caity,* the way people say your name when you're irredeemably naive. Whatever the case, I will be someone who *didn't know* who *meant well.* But I'm not so sure this is true.

I think, looking back, I knew at the airport, while coming here. I must have known, because I saw him there, at the bookshop next to terminal 38D. My father browsing bestsellers in preparation for a long flight, one hand in his pocket, bag slung over his shoulder. He turned his head towards me and I looked down, not recognising him at first. He appeared, after all, not as I knew him—grey hair and a pouch of gut, pleated pants and sensible shirt—but how the public knew him best. Damp sleeves rolled to his elbows, notebook in his top pocket, my age.

But I looked back up—a flicker of recognition—and he was there still, holding my gaze, although I couldn't read his expression. Then, as these things tend to happen, a crowd of Germans walked in front of him, and he was gone. I was left there, stupid, one hand on my suitcase handle, heartbeat hot in my ears.

But I got on the plane and came here. I soon forgot the incident. I was exhausted from my insomnia; it was easy to convince myself it was an odd coincidence, a freak doppelganger. It's not so strange that I was dismissive, I see my father everywhere lately. In the expression of men on the bus, the way chefs suck

KATERINA GIBSON

down their cigarettes in alleys behind restaurants, filter pinched between thumb and forefinger.

If the job requirements were not accurate in the posting they weren't cleared up when I met Marylyn, my employer. I was picked up at the airport by a taxi and taken to the coast, then by boat to Whitsunday Island, where I met Pete with a jeep, who drove me into the cape of the island. Windows of hidden mansions flashed in the sun as we wound through the deep foliage of the forest.

Pete—semi-retired, four kids, five grandkids, more on the way, he told me, fingers crossed—dropped me off at the gates where a far less cheerful man, John, a housekeeper or butler, some combination of the two, greeted me and led me down a drive that came to reveal an elaborate mansion, many-windowed and Greek-terraced, at odds with the trees that hid it from the road. Truthfully, I am still not sure of the specifics of John's job either, although he's pleasant enough, polite, not nosy.

He showed me to my private quarters—he used that phrase, 'private quarters'—which turned out to be a detached bungalow towards the back of the property, plump-looking bed, stovetop, small bathroom. He let me drop off my suitcase and wash my face before insisting that Marylyn urgently wanted to meet me.

Entering the building from the stairs that wound up from the bungalow, we walked first through a corridor that also snaked and turned, labyrinthine, until John led us to an inauspicious door that opened to what I now know as the left wing of the house. There we entered a cavernous dining room, although that's hardly the word for it. This was where she liked to entertain, to throw dinner parties, soirees. Where the bourgeois of the Whitsundays gathered for champagne toasts, where women

196

with impeccable highlights asked after gluten-free aperitifs. But I am being cynical here—in all honesty, I've heard no mention of gluten-free aperitifs. I'm trying to be wary of where I'm heightening the story, making lazy stereotypes, because it would be easy, again, to play the victim. I worry I'm catastrophising. Perhaps many of my colleagues have taken similar jobs, residencies, over the years, the true nature of which are revealed like an unknown rope pulled slowly out of the ocean. Maybe this isn't such a big deal, my anxiety misplaced. Maybe, instead, it's the signs I can read in the water that have put me on edge.

My first thought was that the room was lit by fluorescence. A giant lava lamp is what I thought. My eyes had to adjust to the waves of light dancing across the floor, the plush couches, and the doors that lined the three other walls. Only halfway into the room did it occur to me—perhaps it was the hollow clicking of John's shoes that sounded like water dripping, or maybe I remarked that the light looked just like the refractions of waves on the bottom of a pool. Yes, it was this remark, I think, which made me stop and realise that my impression was not only accurate but entirely correct. The wall that I'd taken for a glass display, or the type of digital artwork popular with the rich and famous, full of abstract moving neon, in fact looked into a pool.

I can't tell you, truthfully, at what point I realised the pool was actually a tank, ceilinged in glass. Maybe this is all a lie, and as soon as I walked in I realised the implications of its emptiness. I'd like to say I didn't know until much later, until after I began my daily expeditions to the reef to collect and document exactly where the specimens were going, and to some extent this is true. That I didn't know why exactly I was there. But, it would not be lying, either, to say I had some idea then, the first time I saw it. Maybe this is why I stared so long, trying to see the furthest edges of the tank, catch the colour sullied in the verdancy of the bush behind it, but finding only the water smudge a deeper blue.

John cleared his throat, holding the door open on the other side of the room. He led me through yet another corridor, then a study which led to stairs, the top of which opened up into a bedroom almost as large as the dining room. Delicate black netting hung from the ceiling, enveloping the bed. Shawls in shades of purple, blue and black blocked out the window. On a mattress the size of a small whale, Marylyn lay half sunken in a mound of pillows of the same colours. It was an odd camouflage event not unlike the cloakfish, made more convincing by her arm held up and over her head, the nook of her elbow covering the top half of her face. If it hadn't been for her two feet, plump like honeydew melons, sticking out at the end of the bed, I mightn't have known she was there.

'She's not feeling very well,' John said.

'Caitlin dear.' This came so quietly from the pile of pillows, I strained to hear her over her dry lips smacking. 'It must be about to storm. I always get a migraine when it's about to storm. Was your trip here okay?'

'Yes, fine, thank you.'

'Good, glad to hear. I'm glad to meet you dear, but you'll have to forgive me. Did John show you your room?'

'Yes.'

'Good, John will look after you. I've got a terrible migraine.'

'It's no problem.'

'It was sunny just before.'

'Yes, it was sunny when I came in.'

'John will look after you.'

I looked at John and he smiled, and motioned me out the door.

'Did you want anything, ma'am?' he asked her as we left. 'A nightcap, some tea?'

'In a bit maybe, yes. Thank you, John. Bring me a nightcap in a bit. And please don't forget to feed Bear.'

After I was escorted back to my room I unzipped my suitcase and unpacked my belongings into the sleek pinewood drawers left empty for me. Marylyn was right; large grey clouds were settled over the tips of the trees, misting the windows. I wasn't to know then how frequently prone to migraines my employer was, nor all the things that triggered them. It wasn't only storms——too hot, too dry, and she'd collapse on the nearest couch, settee, ottoman. Stress and boredom could also set her off, as could dinner when it wasn't adequate, or things weren't going to plan. Once, she got a migraine because there was nothing good on television. The headaches would come in the middle of planning her next party—her hobby—or a wedding, her vocation on the mainland. Though from what I understand she doesn't need the money. Her husband, whose existence I was not aware of at this time and who I still have not met, is apparently the one with money. I can't tell you a single other thing about him. What he does for work, or for fun, nor the degree to which he is aware of my presence in his house—nor, in fact, how often he occupies it himself.

When Marylyn felt the start of a migraine she'd retreat to her bedroom for hours, days sometimes. This, along with her being away for long stretches of time for her job—someplace where she no doubt lives in another modern atrocity—or for elaborate social events around the country, meant that I didn't see much of my employer. Not much at all after that first month, although John and Bear—a bloodhound, when I had been expecting a small yappy thing—were always around. A sad duo, the two of them, John standing in the yard feeding Bear the scraps of his food, both of their jowls wobbling. John in the morning reading the paper that he'd later use to scoop up Bear's damp shit, retching, telling me you don't get used to it.

In the dew of the morning after my arrival, birds up and at it, trees gleaming, leaves erect with life from the early November storm, I sat out the front of my bungalow eating breakfast, my lungs happily filled with petrichor, a scent so familiar to me as to overwhelm and empty my mind, as if to short-circuit it. Marylyn emerged from the doors she threw open with a performative relish and walked down a winding stone path that came to a gazebo. It was impossible not to think of her as floating, the way she walked. Her hands raised to the heavens in greeting. Dressed again—dressed, as I would soon learn, always—in long shawls and skirts that obscured how her feet hit the ground, beads aplenty around her neck, fingers fat with tanzanite. She reached the railing of the gazebo, from which she could survey the sloping property, and looked down at me.

'Darling!' Bear had escaped from the house and came bounding down the stairs that linked to the bungalow. He put his wet nose on my foot and flicked his eyes up at me.

'Did you sleep alright?'

'Yes, well, thank you.' I lied.

'And the storm didn't keep you awake?'

'No, not at all, soothing actually.'

'You'll be going out on the boat today, then.'

'Oh—fantastic.'

'*Eugene.*' She said this name with a French accent. '*Eugene* will take you out for a spin. Oh Bear, be a good boy. He's a good boy. Yes, he likes a good pat. Will you be needing anything?'

'No, I'm fine, thank you.'

'And the breakfast is alright?'

'The jam is delicious.' I took a bite of toast as if to prove it.

Marylyn strode back to the house, calling behind her that she *better get going, then, darling, do ask if you need anything,* and left the doors ajar behind her. I sat there wondering why I hadn't asked her what made her so passionate about having a residential ecologist. Because she was weary of her own environmental footprint and wanted to understand or counteract it? Was it to help protect the reef? Endangered species? What did she care? Were her motives of the guilty or philanthropic kind?

There is a chance I'm superimposing these thoughts onto that moment. That I didn't think this at the time, did not doubt why I had been employed there. That I simply went back to my toast, read the news on my laptop, content to sit there and empty my mind with the smell of the freshly rained-on earth, then got ready for my first day out on the boat. Yes, I'm not so sure I did consider then that I'd been hired not in the interest of conservation and research, but in the same way she'd hire a florist for a wedding.

Jan 11

I fell asleep at my desk last night, so I didn't get to write down what I wanted to—and now something else has come up. Now the thing I thought would happen has happened. This is how these things go. What I was wanting to write about was the reef, starting with my trip out there with Eugene. Who turned out to be from the Sunshine Coast, a few hours south, and as far as I could tell, not holding any pretensions about being French. After breakfast, I took the track at the back of the property, a thin, foot-trodden path that wound steeply beneath a canopy of tall ferns and trees with skeins of moss, before the smell of the ocean approached, and the trees broke down into tufts of shoulder-, then elbow-, then knee-high bushes as the forest reached the edge of the beach, as if it might lean down to drink at high tide. At the shoreline there was a long wooden jetty that reached out over some rocks to a deep pool where a boat—not a modest research vessel, as I'd encountered on similar trips, but a small yacht—was docked, a young man sitting in it.

'G'day. Caitlin?' The man held out his hand to both shake mine and assist me onto the boat. 'Name's Eugene. Nice to meet you.'

He had dimples and tan of someone who'd grown up in the surf, hair and skin the same bronze colour, eyebrows shards of straw. There was something carefree about the way he held his body. He took me around the immediate area, near tourist dive sites and the still-blooming reef, which looked, as we sailed over it, like an underwater circus, colours blurring.

On that first trip, Eugene told me how he had got the job as my boat mate, how he'd taken Marylyn out on a private tour—he usually toured small groups, showing the reef to loud Americans, mainly, who asked about shark attacks and never wore enough sunscreen. He pointed out turtles, telling them about the threats the reef faced (microplastics, climate change, corporate destruction). Marylyn had taken a liking to him, offered him the job on the spot. That was a few months ago.

Once we were out over the ocean, away from the shallow reef, going faster, he whooped with genuine joy, and I could see why Marylyn was so fond of him. Although, now I think about it, this can't be right; I would only learn that later.

Eugene asked me if I wanted to dive or snorkel, and where seemed appealing.

I asked him to take me somewhere remote—away from the tourists at least. Remote but shallow, I wanted to snorkel. I always prefer to snorkel—less confining, more freedom, more control—although diving is an occupational hazard. In the meantime, I looked inside at the equipment. The boat was filled, brimming, with different-sized tubs. Some smaller, made to keep fighting fish in suburban kitchens. Others, fit for a dozen smallish tropical fish. One in particular, long and flat, might bring to mind a manta ray or a sunfish, but my first thought was of the cloakfish.

I realise I've yet to describe my specialisation. I study the cloakfish or the *Vitreus mola*. My fascination with it comes in part from its rarity; there has been, to date, only a handful of documented sightings, two of which I was present for.

Three, as of today.

The thing that makes the cloakfish so difficult to identify is its almost complete invisibility. Its ability to camouflage itself is astonishing. Amateur enthusiasts are quick to liken it to the cuttlefish, the rockfish, octopi, and other fish with camouflaging abilities, but this is not, as I have outlined in many papers, accurate. The cuttlefish et al. can be identified by their texture and their close imitation of their surroundings. The cloakfish, however, is entirely translucent, or appears to be. It is like looking through a recently Windexed window. *Vitreus mola:* glass mill-stone. Glass flatfish.

The first cloakfish I saw was off Fraser Island—on the trip where I was photographed with the turtle hatchlings. I was there with another cloakfish specialist I knew and two friends in similar fields. There'd been rumours of a sighting in the area.

We spent days out on our boat, a little metal dingy, staring at the one spot for hours, waiting for a flash of gills. At the time, this was considered the only way to find it, waiting for three disembodied gills to open in the middle of the ocean. Ghostgills, the locals called the fish. There are other ways to spot it now, if you know how. The most rigorous and tiring of which is what I, in part, have been up to the last two or so months: documenting what fish are inhabiting a specific part of the reef and how the ecosystem changes over a period of time, say a week, then rinse and repeat. The cloakfish's effect on other species is interesting. Some small fish one might consider prey seem happy to hide in their coral homes for extended periods while the cloakfish floats above them, keeping a shrewd eye on it like they would any other predator. Other fish, however, appear not to be able to see the cloakfish and are happy to graze coral and smaller fish in its presence—perhaps like us, they can't really comprehend it. Often entire colonies are eaten by an invisible predator. Others still, small enough to swim beneath the cloakfish, become confused by its underbelly, which, unlike the view we are privy to from above, looks as if the colours of the reef have been caught and reflected off its strange body. These fish will act disorientated and confused—as though they have entered a hall of mirrors and become dizzy. What I'm getting at is, if someone—and in this case I am that someone—were to document a part of the reef and the behaviour of the fish there for a concentrated period of time they could, I could, hypothetically, *track* the cloakfish. Finding it has been likened to the way astronomers identify black holes. This type of research and documentation is where most of the evidence for the cloakfish's existence comes from. Although there are still plenty of sceptics.

It would be rare, in other words, in the win-the-lottery-twice sense, for four friends to simply come across one on a boat, whatever our collective qualifications. But this is exactly what happened. It was on our third day in the one spot, I was snorkelling off the boat with Evie, the other cloakfish special-ist. She had just tapped me on the hand—her signal to say she was going up—when I saw it. The gape of three gills, the water sliced open, thrice, to reveal the dark interior of the fish—a vent opening momentarily to another dimension. I grabbed her hand, squeezing it tight, pointing with the other. We stayed like that for some minutes, me pointing when it happened again, and I heard her gasp underwater. We surfaced, Evie coughing and trying not to splash, and called Eamon and Teddy over. Since they did not specialise in cloakfish, they were treating the trip as more of a holiday than an expedition and the two of them were mid-beer, cackling. We shushed them and motioned towards the edge of the boat. I reached for Eamon's hand, pulling him closer, and pointed. The four of us, two in the water, two in the boat, stayed there staring at the coral when it happened. The cloak-fish swam off. Something they don't do often; their camouflage is threatened when they move so quickly. Although mostly you can't tell any difference in the body of the fish—there might be a slight ripple, but nothing that you wouldn't already think of as disturbances in the water, albeit in strange ways, counter to the current. However, whenever the fish does move it loses—just around its edges—its ability to colour, and you can see its outline undulate. We saw, the four of us, the true scope of it, round with a long tail—not, again, unlike a manta ray—and huge, almost two metres in length. But I'm getting everything out of order. This is not the thing I wanted to tell you.

When I first came here and began to understand the real nature of my employment, I believed that my specialty in the cloakfish was a large part of the reason I was hired. Not, as I had originally been lead to believe, because Marylyn had any specific interest in my research per se, and was philanthropically funding the sought-after residency most ecologists dreamed of, but because of the jurisdiction it grants me. As to track *Vitreus mola* requires not only a thorough knowledge of the fish, but a comprehensive understanding of the species and environment that co-exist with it—their behaviour, their patterns. It grants you the ability to collect a broad array of species.

Bear has been whining to be let in for some time now so he can sleep on my bed. I'm going to let him in and join him. I feel for once that I can fall asleep easily, and have to take rest when it comes.

Jan 13

I said before that I saw my employer the most in the first month or so I stayed here. I believe now that this was intentional. That her drop-ins were to make sure I would co-operate.

Initially, I saw Marylyn in the mornings, when she'd sweep dramatically out of the main house, throwing the doors open, inhaling with a performative relish, and then in the same voice she used each time, saying, 'Darling, so nice to see you,' her tone as if finding me at the table outside the bungalow with my coffee was a delightful little treat. She'd ask how I was enjoying the work, chat idly, say *the weather's nice today, looks like it might rain, you look tired, darling.* Eventually, though, these morning meetings gave way to far less frequent dinners. I'd been there about a fortnight or so when she came out one morning, feigned her usual surprise at seeing me, declared the day beautiful and invited me to dinner. Bear was already with me, head resting on my lap.

'Oh, he's taken a liking to you, hasn't he dear?'

I looked up from my notebook and smiled.

'I'm having some other friends over to dinner tonight. You will come, won't you? You can tell them all about your work; they are *very* interested.'

I agreed, and after telling me to wear something nice—'A dress or something, darling, you're always in these trousers'—she left.

As packing evening wear for this job hadn't occurred to me, at dinnertime I put on my green linens—flowing pants, button-up shirt—and went to join her.

I had not yet ventured into the house alone and on my way to dinner I became lost in its strange layout, finding myself in a loop of corridors that led not where I remembered them going, but to more rooms or hallways that I'd already walked through.

When I finally found the room, it was accidental, and I thought, as I entered from a different perspective, I had made yet another mistake. The couches were gone and in their place a dinner table was set up, pointing lengthways towards the tank. Although the sun had set, the water was emanating an artificial, otherworldly glow. Marylyn sat at the head of the table, facing the tank. On either side of her were an older man and woman. A married couple, I would soon learn. Eugene was seated next to the woman. She motioned to the empty chair opposite him and I sat down.

'You look nice, dear,' Marylyn said.

'Thank you.'

'This is Neil and Sharon. The friends I was telling you about who are *most* interested in your work.'

'Yes, *fascinating,* what you do, fascinating,' said Neil.

I tried to give Eugene a small smile, but he was looking down at the table.

'The fish are simply lovely.' This was Sharon smiling at me.

'Pardon?' I said.

She cleared her throat, raised her eyebrows and nodded towards the tank.

I'm unsure why I didn't notice immediately; perhaps the company and new set-up distracted me, or maybe I was too preoccupied attempting to make a decent first impression. But I think most probably I was, knowing the depth of the tank, subconsciously averting my eyes. Despite my occupation, I have always found large bodies of water intimidating. It is impossible, after all, when faced with the black drop-off of the deep ocean not to consider your own body in it. It can snatch me anywhere, this feeling of vertigo. Like John with Bear's shit: I've never got used to it.

Once, on a different trip, a different year, further north, where the reef is dead (which is disconcerting in another way entirely), after drifting off into thought for few moments, I found myself not above the safety of the reef, but above a sudden drop, the unceasing blackness of the pit beneath, around, enveloping me. I felt my body like an underwater maggot, tiny, pale and squirming. My tank stopped working. I began to panic, swallowing the sea in anxious gulps.

When Eamon pulled me from the water he was laughing. 'Jesus, I thought you'd seen a shark. What happened, did you piss your pants?'

I lay on the floor of the boat, deep breathing, felt between my legs. Once I caught my breath, I said, 'I might have.' My tank was working fine.

Squid, this is what Eamon called me. Scaredy squid.

When I was younger I held—theoretically—an interest in deep-water creatures. Every birthday my dad, appearing at my childhood house like a lost traveller looking for food and water, would pull me into a sweeping hug, spin me around and put me down, before handing me a new book of animals that glowed and bared their terrifying teeth in the midnight water. 'A book of critters for my critter,' he would say. I would spend hours drawing angler fish, floor-dwelling crabs, small, fluorescent aliens on sheets of black-blue paper to give to him, before he would again leave, not to be seen until the wind—his work—swept him back our way. In practice, I discovered that deep-sea exploration was not an option for me—I was not cut out for it. I've been thinking lately maybe I am not so cut out for this job, either.

Forgive me: back at the dinner table, staring into the tank, I couldn't see anything at first. Then there were small colourful movements in the shadows. Of course, the specimens I'd scooped gently from their coral homes, tipped into their appropriate containers. I wonder how this must feel, swaying to the move-ment of the water in the tank, itself on a boat bobbing to the rhythm of the ocean—I wonder if the fish feel some gyroscopic effect. If fish get vertigo.

'We just thought they'd be much happier in here than that little boat,' she said. 'Don't you think?'

I didn't say anything, didn't look at her, just continued to stare at the fish.

'Wait.' A butterfly fish had swum right up to the glass, then another, and another. Five in total. On the boat, I'd collected only two. I'd only been able to find two. I had documented them, with the others, then placed them in tanks to be released back into the reef, as you're legally meant to. I felt my fingers grow warm as I released that she knew that—of course she did. I told Eugene all about it, my intentions with the fish. And he had offered to release them, said that was his job—although, I realised then, he had not specified where. Before that dinner, I told Eugene everything.

Well, not everything.

Another butterfly fish swam past.

'Where did you get them?'

'We got them off the boat dear, you know that.'

'When did you get them?' I said this to Eugene, who would not look at me.

'Yes, it's amazing how quickly they breed, isn't it?' Marylyn said.

I turned to look at her; she stared back, her mouth corners raised and pulled inward toward her. I could see the fine cracks in her lipstick.

John walked in, three plates in his hands. The cook followed with another two plates and a wine bucket, in which sat a popped champagne bottle, misting a trail behind her like a cosmic snail, and began to tell us about the food. Marylyn pursed her lips at me a second longer then turned to smile, a real smile, with teeth, at John. 'Oh, lovely, lovely.'

'Incredible, truly incredible.' This was Neil, although I was unsure if he was talking about the butterfly fish or the linguine.

John poured the champagne and Marylyn raised her glass. 'To Caitlin!' she said. 'For her magnificent skills and dedication to the conservation of the reef.'

'To Caitlin.'

'Caitlin.'

'Caitlin.'

I raised my glass and looked at Eugene, but he still refused to look at me, fixing his gaze on some distant point in the tank. Waves of blue light rippled over his beautiful face.

That night, when I did at last fall asleep, I dreamt of the house, corridors that led into more corridors, water lapping at my feet.

Jan 18

It hasn't stopped storming for three days now; I haven't been able to go back out to the reef. Bear has stayed with me for most of it, whining on my bed, unless he is having dinner or shitting somewhere inside the main house on her shagpile carpet, which makes me love him even more.

The dinner I was just writing about did not end there, although my ability to stay lucid almost did. I spent the rest of the meal anxiously chewing pasta, which I threw up just as anxiously later. I answered Neil or Sharon's questions in polite but short sentences. Eugene made up for my demeanour by being his booming and entertaining self—with everyone but me. At one point, towards the end of the meal, he actually looked back at me, but his expression was blank, more serious than I thought he was capable of.

But maybe I'm projecting. Maybe he was unaware he'd been avoiding eye contact, for the next second, he was smiling at Sharon, laughing at something she said. Maybe he was never avoiding me in the first place. I'm still not sure where to place him, Eugene. Whether he was naive or cunning or vulnerable, or if he had other motives that evaded me. I'm aware that he is not someone you naturally assign intelligence to. Whether he was easy to manipulate or just liked to appear that way.

I can't place a lot of things. How much of this I knew at the time, how much I only realised later. Recently I have been thinking that if I were the woman I wanted to be, none of this would have happened. If I were more like my dad, this would never have happened. If I had absorbed what he had wanted to teach me, about how to act on the environment from a position of care, instead of how I have become, porous, absorbed by my surroundings until I dissolve into them. If I had learnt to act on, rather than be acted upon. That is to say, if I weren't such a coward—which is what people must think of me.

I still haven't told you the things I set out to write. But I am getting there. Maybe this is why I'm taking so long, because I am afraid. A scared squid.

Jan 18 cont.

I was getting antsy. I needed to leave the bungalow, stretch my legs; damn the rain. I went for a walk down the path through the forest, turning off from my usual route. The forest-cum-bush of the island is dense and eerie with constant echo. A bird was shrieking in the distance, I didn't recognise the call, or rather could not assign it to one species, for although it came from the same unseen spot in the canopy, it let out myriad trills and chirps. I supposed then it was a lyrebird. Creatures, my father once told me, which were like living ghosts, mimicking seasonal birds that had moved onto the south, passing down the generations songs of long-extinct species, haunting the forest with ancient birdsong. It would make sense that lyrebirds are here; I'm not sure how it hasn't occurred to me before. Sometimes at night, as I feel the weight of Bear's body on my feet, or see his breath fogging the glass door, I think I hear his distant barking.

After some time on my walk, an hour or so at a turn in the path, I stepped forward and saw five trees grouped together in a very particular arrangement. The way they lined up triggered a memory in me and I was suddenly smelling not the lush wetness of the place, but the sweat of a crowd of strangers. Trees very like these were projected onto the back of a theatre, the rest of the stage dark. It was a strange industry event, it must have been, with readings from papers, poems, essays, the performing of songs. Yes, I'm remembering now, the event was marketed as a meeting of the arts and science, Thoughts on the Anthropocene, Thoughts of the Future. Something like that, don't quote me. The theatre and adjoining bar were full of academics, ecologists, writers, young artists. I felt, there on the path, the murmur of an audience dim as the lights did, the shiver of Eamon's thumb caressing my neck as he withdrew his arm from the back of my seat. We'd gone out for intermission, secured glasses of red, talked to acquaintances. There was something so distinctive about the grouping of the trees in the forest that I thought, just for a moment, this must have been where the photo in the theatre had been taken. In this locale, from this exact angle, in this season. I was completely convinced, standing in the forest, that I was staring at the trees I had seen in a photograph. Perhaps I thought this because of how intently I'd stared at the photo that night.

In the theatre, a singer had this image projected behind him as he set up—a MIDI keyboard, foot pedal, microphone, xylophone. I remember the sight of the xylophone alarmed me at the time and I braced myself. Rightfully so, it turned out. As he began to sing—or wail, to be more accurate—I saw Eamon from the corner of my eye, a ridiculous grin on his face. I shifted my gaze from the singer to the photo of trees and for the next fifteen minutes concentrated on not laughing.

Eamon did not do as well as me and as the song went on—as the earnest wails became louder, as the keyboard drone swelled— he shook with silent giggles. At some point I extended my hand to grip his knee, and he bit his knuckles; I felt my emotions turn, continued to stare at the trees not in order to keep from laughing, but to prevent myself yelling at Eamon. This is what the trees reminded me of, standing there in the forest. That event with Eamon. Furious with him for making the night so much harder. Furious with myself for bringing him.

When the song finished at last, we both relaxed, my grip on his knee, his hand from his mouth. The relaxing was premature, though: the singer had stopped only for a dramatic pause. He sent out one last resonant note from his synthesiser, a sound like a laser beam firing. Eamon, likewise, shot out an abrupt burst of laughter.

'I can't believe you,' I said later that night, palms pressed over my eyes.

'Oh come on, he was taking the piss.'

'I don't think he was.'

'He had to be.'

'Art is important.'

'I didn't say it wasn't.'

I pressed the heels of my hands harder into my eyes, eyelids bursting with light.

'Are we going to call that art?' he said more quietly, less sure of himself.

I moved my hands off my eyes, lounge room erupting in dancing worms, and looked down at him, fuming. 'You're supposed to be the responsible one, remember?'

He reached his hand up and placed it on my stomach, a warm touch where I was expecting cold. 'Caitlin, he wasn't helping. If anything, he just made it easier for conservatives to call us hippies.'

We looked at each other in silence. I went to move his hand off but he stopped me, looking at me with a serious frown on his face. He reached out his other hand to my face, paused, and made the synthesiser's laser-beam sound.

In front of those trees in the forest, I collapsed with laughter, as both of us had on the couch. I fell to my knees laughing, unable to stop, and remained there despite the rain, my eyes tight and heavy in my head, thinking how not all our fights ended like that one, my laughing turning into crying, unsure of the distinction between the too.

I'm not sure how long I knelt there in the mud of the forest floor, water streaming down my back. Nor which way I went when I got up, or how I found myself back here.

When I got to the bungalow I was soaked through and freezing. After a hot shower I fell asleep naked, and woke to my covers flipped, the sheet lying on top of the doona. Lately I've been having strange dreams, corridors filling with water, a glow in strange heaving light, something swimming towards me in the shallows, my father looking on solemnly from a doorway, which, as I approach, he closes behind himself and can't be found when I open it. I'm messing up the bedding in odd ways, confusing dreams with reality.

I'm dressed and at the desk now, but I have let myself get distracted. The sun has set. Bear is at my feet. I have missed a lot, forgotten things, misplaced them. I'm going to try to tell you everything. Let me think.

Jan 18 cont.

I have said that it has not stopped raining for days, and that's prevented me from working, from going to the reef. But the truth is, rain doesn't always stop me, and hasn't always since I've been here. I've begun to postpone working when I can. I don't know what else to do. It was raining that day, when we saw the cloakfish, me and Eugene, or when I saw it and I swear he did too. Raining lightly, water shivering in rings. I was in the water, a wet suit, diving that day—there is no use snorkelling in foul weather. The summer, which we were in the heat of, started to sweat. Sun, caught between the water and the clouds, making the air thick. I think we welcomed the rain, the two of us. Although I'd become hesitant with Eugene after that first initial dinner, I'd warmed to him a bit again, relaxed. Convinced myself he was just doing his job. That he didn't have any choice—and who was I anyway, to judge someone else's morals.

That isn't to say I confided in him all the time. What I did tell him though, I shouldn't have.

It's become harder as my insomnia has become worse to make sense of things; I am still not sure what is right and what is not. What I told him was after the first dinner, but this instance I'm wanting to relate was after the second dinner see—or no, the second dinner was shortly after this instance when I began to write all this down. I'm confusing time lines again. I'm going to begin again.

Jan 18 cont.

About a month, a month and a half, into my stay here, was when I went to the second dinner, or at least it was the second time a dinner had stuck in my mind. I accounted for the time the house would swallow me but to my surprise found my way through the halls easily and arrived early. I was staring at the dining table, my back turned to the tank, when the door opened and Eugene walked in. He stopped when he saw me, his blush blooming— cheeks to ears to neck—purple in the light.

I turned away from him towards the tank. There were new additions, of course. But not just fish. The tank was filled with debris—planks of wood and seaweed. A fish I had collected the previous day weaved through some seagrass.

'Jesus fucking Christ, Eugene.'

The door opened and guests entered. Two couples this time. Not Neil and Sharon, but of the same ilk. The dinner table was set for seven, and as they introduced themselves they mistook my anger—my fingers shaking, my voice catching—for shyness. I heard them remarking on my introversion. Marylyn, I then saw, had entered without my noticing, and we all sat around the table.

Now, see, here is where I am getting mixed up: I am confusing two dinners, one of them happened after we saw the fish and one before. But I can't determine which was which. In the first one, perhaps I was kinder to Eugene, and he would not have blushed so easily as he walked in, but then again if the first dinner was the one shortly after he placed all the debris in the tank, I would have been furious. Perhaps I am wrong in all of this, and had convinced myself Eugene was responsible for neither the extra fish nor the adornments.

I'm not sure, but I'm going to go ahead anyway. We sat as before: Marylyn at the end of the table, facing the tank, the two couples opposite one another, myself and Eugene at the far end. We were halfway through a Thai duck curry when she said, 'And Caitlin specialises in a very intriguing fish, you must know.' She was speaking to the woman seated next to me, who wore dramatic glasses, but had raised her voice over the chatter of the table, so that everyone turned towards me. She continued to be preoccupied with her duck curry.

I looked over at Eugene for help, but he only bit his bottom lip. I looked at the woman with the glasses and smiled, and began to explain about the cloakfish, when the man next to her interrupted me.

'*Huh.*' Curry was clinging to his moustache.

'Sorry?'

'You're not serious, are you?'

I remember I smiled again. It happens sometimes, this response from strangers. 'No, no I'm afraid I am.' He let out another huff, then said to Marylyn, 'You've outdone yourself this time.' He looked at her.

'Pardon?'

She stopped eating to give him a tight-lipped smile. 'You would know all about it, George, would you?'

George's shoulders began to rise up and down in hiccups. There was a prolonged pause, and I realised he was not hiccupping, but stifling giggles.

'Listen . . .' I started to assert myself, to assure George of the cloakfish's existence. That, while his understanding of the fish was no doubt a result of one too many online jokes, the species has for seven years now been accepted as a real one.

As I spoke though, my frown was perhaps too deep, or I raised my voice too much, because I was again interrupted. His wife, sitting opposite him, next to Eugene, said even more loudly, 'This curry is *delicious*.' The women with the dramatic glasses and her husband agreed, and after that, the dinner more or less returned to normal. Although that didn't stop George, whenever there was a lull in conversation, asking with a smirk if I also hunted yetis, or when would I be off to the loch. But the tension more or less subsided as we were served dessert and more wine. It wasn't until near the end, when Marylyn, more collected than before, said, 'Well, we'll just have to prove you wrong, George, when we have the cloakfish here, won't we?'

She said this without looking at me, instead smiling over at Eugene, and then, angling her head back, mouth agape, she finished off her wine in one swig.

Yes, that's right, I'm remembering now. What I got wrong is the beginning, there weren't that many more fish or objects in the tank. I had not started the dinner angry, but become upset during the course of it. I remember this because George remarked, looking at the tank, 'Not at this rate you won't.' And then he asked me, 'How long have you been here?' He laughed again. 'Pulled the wool over on this one, haven't you? Good on you,' he said, and winked at me. Truthfully, at this point there was a considerable number of fish in the tank already, but due to its vast expanse, they swam into sight only occasionally. Certainly, there were more than I'd handled myself. But I can see, now, how the tank would look to an outsider: empty.

'George, really, is this necessary?' That was his wife. A thin woman, who'd at last stopped flirting with Eugene long enough for her husband's behaviour to embarrass her.

There was another prolonged silence. I looked again at Eugene, who stared at George, bemused.

I am remembering now: the feeling in my stomach. That feeling when Marylyn mentioned the fish. But even then, I don't think I took her seriously. At the time, I figured she made that comment about getting a cloakfish only because of her irritation at George. That she was aware my ability to find the cloakfish had been greatly handicapped now my specimens were being nicked, and that she was far more interested in this—building her collection—than completing it with the cloakfish. That she had no interest, in fact, in a fish that is invisible, because it could not be neatly converted into a symbol of status. I certainly did not—do not now—believe she was fascinated with the cloakfish's ability to blend almost perfectly into its environment, or with what this says about its nature and about those, like myself, who are drawn to it. That it was hard not to take the cloakfish being ridiculed and ignored, personally. It wasn't until I saw the pattern that I remembered Marylyn's remark and began to fear she was serious. I began to fear, too, the more cynical aspects of the cloakfish, an invisible predator who no one pays attention to—what it means to swim so easily into a place of advantage, be able to take whatever you want while people look right through you.

Eugene cleared his throat. 'So how do you know Marylyn?' He directed this to the woman with the glasses, but it was George who answered.

'Marylyn? We're friends with Henry, her husband, who's been so rude as to not join us, again, I noticed.'

'He's very busy tonight, I'm sorry.' Marylyn had barely whispered this and when I looked up she'd closed her eyes and was pressing a forefinger to her temple. A tear pooled in her left eye, just one, from the outer corner, then ran down her face and dripped off her chin.

'Marylyn, are you alright?' This was the woman with the glasses.

'Oh yes, I'm perfectly fine. A small headache is all. Perfectly fine, dear, it's not what you think. Coming down with a migraine, perhaps.'

John, who had appeared at her side, took her elbow and helped her out of her chair, then without addressing any of us guided her out of the room.

'Now really.' George's wife, blue light making her skinniness morbid. 'Was that necessary?'

But George only started laughing again, his head now in his hands. Eugene and I looked at one another, and the six of us sat there for some minutes as George calmed himself. When John slipped back into the room, through the opposite door he'd exited from, he said Marylyn was ill and, he was terribly sorry, but when we were ready to collect our jackets and bags, to please leave as quietly as possibly so her headache wouldn't upset into a migraine.

George got up with a loud scrape. Then, sheepish, he whispered, 'Sorry.' He turned to me. 'Sorry, love, I didn't mean to upset you.' He paused, twitched his mouth, and said to the empty seat at the end of the table, 'I didn't want to upset anyone.'

The two couples left, John accompanying them to the front door.

Eugene and I left through a separate corridor. On our way out, down a hallway that opened out at a sharp angle from the one were walking down, I thought I saw an unfamiliar shoe retreating into a room, heard the click of a lock. But I hear and see a lot that I'm unsure of—people coming and going, a conversation stopping as I walk by, noise coming from rooms that are empty when I open them, the roar of a boat in the middle of the night. Eugene asked why I'd stopped, and when I didn't answer, he took my hand and led me out of the house.

Thinking about it now, I'm not sure how I got these two dinners so confused but I do get everything mixed up. There is a chance that the two couples did not come together at all, but were at separate dinners. For instance, I remember that the other couple talked at length about their fondness for stand-up paddleboarding, how it made them feel youthful again, but I can't place when this happened.

At least this much is clear to me now: these two dinners happened on either side of us seeing the cloakfish, and therefore must have occurred on either side of the new year. And there was another instance when the two of us, Eugene and me, met with Marylyn. Yes, this makes sense. The Christmas lunch.

Yes, we had Christmas lunch between those two dinners, Eugene, me, John, Bear. In the shade of the gazebo. More of a brunch, I suppose: croissants and grapes, eggs and mimosas.

I must have laughed a little out loud at Bear frolicking in the grass, because John said, 'Yes, he's having a good time isn't he.' It took me a second to realise he was talking about Bear, and I was about to say something, to pull him out of his conversation, when Marylyn turned to me and said, 'And Caitlin, have you seen they've put together a special on your dad? Airing tomorrow, Boxing Day special. Channel Ten I think, but they're also doing a one-off cinema release on the mainland cinema, since he spent so much of his time working on the reef. I could arrange for you to go if you like.'

I took a sip of my mimosa, felt the sting of my saliva glands. I had known about the special of course—some hatchet job someone had thrown together from previous footage with dollar signs lighting up their eyes, no doubt half premade in anticipation of his death. Dad would have been appalled. I'd declined politely to be interviewed for it, although I'd had half a mind not to be—polite, that is. The shiny invite to the premiere I never had any intention of going to was somewhere in the bowels of my bag, although it is interesting I ended up in a place so close to it. My father had three ex-wives, and no other children, so it had fallen to me to deal with the impossible requests from everyone wanting to benefit from his name. In the end I made the lawyers deal with the bulk of it, all I did was tell the documentary makers that if they had any sense they would send their profits to the environmental organisations that fought the coal ports and frackers that threatened the livelihood of the reef— the cause my father had dedicated the last decades of his life to.

The last time I had visited him, I woke in the middle of the night needing the bathroom, and found him awake in his study as I passed it. He was staring off through a window. I asked him why he was up and he rubbed his eyes and said he'd been having trouble sleeping lately. He claimed his arthritis was keeping him up, but then, after a small pause, he turned to me and asked me what it meant, all the work he'd done, when the effects of the people who did not care for the reef would be felt long after his presence had gone.

I shrugged, trying to get away from him, desperate for the bathroom. He saw me jiggling and threw his head back in a booming Australian laugh. This is what people always get wrong when they imitate him, narrating their surroundings with a clipped English accent. In reality his time here by the reef, by me, had changed him, his mouth opening slackly on his 'Y's and 'I's, laughing the way only men who've spent time in Australian pubs can. He said for me to go on then, go back to bed.

Maybe it is not so peculiar I am here at all. Maybe it is entirely understandable that in my grief I have gravitated towards the place he was most associated with, to feel his presence here, before the reef too is gone, and the only places he and it will haunt are our collective imaginations, before that too leaves us, footage of him in his khakis, the opulent colours of this underwater kingdom corrupting, as time erodes everything but devastation.

To Marylyn on Christmas Day I said, 'That's alright. Thank you, though.'

Eugene did not look surprised. Neither did John. This was the first time she had mentioned him. The first time she had indicated that she knew he was my father. I should have known better. I am, if not underqualified, perhaps a shade too young to have got this position: mid-career, the posting had said. I can see now that if the job were legitimate I would not have been taken on. That it belongs to someone older. Someone who wanted to study the reef to understand how human destruction was affecting their species—someone like Eamon, I'm saying, who never would have let himself do what I have done, what I have convinced myself is okay to do.

'Alright, dear. He's a favourite of mine, you know, I've watched all his stuff, all of it.' Then Marylyn turned back to Eugene and began another anecdote.

Although I'm an adult, and a child of divorce, and had spent many Christmases apart from my father before, it occurred me that this was the first time I was experiencing Christmas and he was not.

Marylyn addressed me again. 'I admired him very much, you know. He was a great man.' She smiled at me then, and for once her lips didn't contract into thin lines.

Jan 20

I woke to the sound of the kettle yawning. Stovetop rattling. I burnt my thumb and forefinger on the lever. I feel odd and light and lucid. I don't remember falling asleep again, but the jug was almost empty when I ran to turn it off. It's getting worse, this insomnia, I'm beginning to have fits of paralysis. The first time I woke this morning I'd been dreaming of my father. I was lying in bed on my back and I couldn't move. I felt a weight on my legs and, although I could not see it, I knew a gigantic lyrebird had put her claw on the bed. She came over the horizon of my body, claws oddly soft, like paws, padding to rest on my breasts, large green eyes looking right at me. I knew then that I was dreaming and willed myself to wake, but my arms were stuck at my sides by this deep weight on my chest. If I could just move my hand, I knew, I would wake and she would stop moving her beak towards mine. Her flesh was not right; it was not feathered but aquatic, thick smooth rubber—porpoise, dolphin—she was not flecked with black and white, but with jagged purple. Her breath damp-smelling. From the crack under the doorway the room began to fill with water. My finger twitched and I gasped awake, sitting up. The weight lifted from my chest but I still couldn't move my arms: I'd cocooned the sheet around my body. Somehow the top blanket had stayed in place. Panicking, I struggled out of the knotted sheet, scaring myself and Bear, who yelped when I swept him off the bed, not realising he was there.

Flinging the door open, I ran towards the forest; my foot snapped a cluster of twigs, I gasped. Not at the pain—I'd startled a colony of bats. In the morning dusk it looked as if the entire canopy had lifted off in a choir of shrieks.

Breathing, sweating, watching the mass freckle and lengthen, I stood there until they became a thin trail, a road above the trees, then went inside to boil the jug. Full circle. This is not how I imagined I would be spending my time here, hoping the rain wouldn't stop, dreaming of my father.

I have been dreaming of him since that evening with Eugene. It was Boxing Day. Marylyn was gone, as was John. He'd taken his small amount of leave to see his grand-nieces and nephews on the mainland—that was the only information I'd gotten from him. That and the fact that lyrebirds don't live this far north. 'Not entirely unheard of but very very unlikely.' John is a bit of an amateur bird watcher, it turns out, one of those things you develop at a certain age. It's bird watching or gardening, from what I understand. I'd spent the day walking, I went down in the morning to where the boat, now absent, was usually docked. Eugene wasn't around and I walked on. The water glittered in the sun; the coral was vivid, bursting. I was not, for once, seeing only future fossils, was not thinking of the stretches of bleached reef, brittle and lifeless, reaching up through black water. A ghost reef, I have watched slip under a boat, dissolve into backwash. I don't have to tell you about those memories. They are inseparable from the images we have all seen. Of eerie dead coral and dark water. It exists collectively, this picture of devastation.

Although I do wonder now, why the water was always, in my memory, so dark, like a storm was always coming. That Boxing Day the sun was bright, a single fluffy cloud, embarrassed it had shown up. The sea was a pristine green stillness. At one point I plunged into it in my underwear, frog-paddling my way over the reef. A galaxy of starfish gleamed below me, peach-coloured, some as big as my head. But I did not think of their fate, the acidification of the ocean that was dissolving entire species of them, only admired their strange sponge-like skin as I swam over them. I got out and ate the food I'd packed, napped in the shade and read a while, went back in the water again, turning to alternate the cool of the water with the heat of the sun on my front and back. A blissful day with the marine creatures.

Before the sun began to set, I made my way back to my bungalow in time for the television special. I'd avoided thinking about it all day—I'd avoided any thinking all day—but I told myself I could just put it on in the background, heat up dinner, curl up on the couch. On the way I saw that the boat was back and I called out to Eugene, but he didn't answer and when I let myself onto the boat it was empty.

When I got to the bungalow, he was leaning against the door, same green shirt as the day before, hair wet.

I know that in recounting events I have not always been reliable, that I have mixed things up. That it is obviously nonsense to claim I've always remembered dialogue accurately, but I do remember what Eugene said to me that evening.

First he said, leaning on my door, 'Come in.' Then he opened the door with his hand behind him.

Steam was licking out of the bathroom doorway. A wet towel— my wet towel—was flung over the back of a chair. I scoffed, jaw open at him. He slung a grin at me.

'I needed a shower.'

'With my towel, did you?'

'Sorry.' His face was serious again, and he looked worried as I sat on the couch in front of the television, legs stretched out.

'Right, anything else you need? Food, shelter, a night cap?'

He laughed. 'Gonna turn on the telly?'

I looked out through the glass door at Bear in the yard. 'I need to feed the dog.'

'I came to watch it with you.'

I got off the couch to collect the can of dog food John had given me the day before. He'd said he could organise to have Bear looked after but he thought I wouldn't mind, and of course

I didn't. I spooned the sludge into his bowl, whistled, and Bear came running.

I went back into the lounge. 'What if I wanted to be alone?'

'Do you?'

I sat down on the couch but didn't stretch out my legs. After a second, Eugene sat beside me.

'I've always wanted to be able to do that.'

'Feed the dog?' I hit the remote then muted the sound.

'Whistle.'

'You can't whistle?'

He tilted his head back, made a lemon nipple out of his lips, and began to blow, too harshly, through a too-small hole.

'Well, you're going about it all wrong.'

'Any pointers?'

'Don't even know where to start.'

'I can do this, though.' He stuck his tongue out and it twisted into curls.

'Okay, no. Gross.'

The doco had started. I unmuted to a grainy shot from the '70s of a lemur, before the camera panned out to my father, young—my age. He looked from the monkey to the camera and began to narrate. *In Madagascar, the island off the east coast . . .* So, they were going to do it chronologically then. This was his first, if not his first big one. He met his first wife, Angelika, the following year, on a trip to South Africa and divorced her the next. He didn't meet my mother for years. She was probably still a teenager then, come to think of it.

This was mostly it: clips of him in various states of ruggedness and then decay. Young and lanky; flamingos in the tropics;

birds nesting in New Zealand; ad break; as he gained muscle and depth through his thirties; tigers in Asia; bobcats in America; ad break; the Great Barrier Reef; salt and pepper beard; lone eagles; foxes in the north; ad break; the weirdness of flightless island birds; the Great Barrier Reef again. Not far from here a fish, a deep movement in my bowels *if nothing is done, soon they won't be found in the wild.*

In my peripheral vision, I saw Eugene, his head resting back, swivel his neck to look at me. 'I'm sorry,' he said.

'Don't worry about the towel, it's fine.'

'Not about the towel.'

I turned to face him. 'They aren't anymore.'

'What?' His forehead crumpled.

'They aren't found in the wild anymore. I knew someone who studied them.'

I turned back to the TV. The next scene showed a different reef now. Another fish I recognised: small, half orange, half purple. 'That's the fish.'

'The fish that what?' Eugene, forehead crumpled again, confused.

'That's the best fish to help you identify a cloakfish.'

'Really?'

'Yeah, I wish there were more of them here. It can't make that specific purple—on the front half of its body.'

'Oh, weird.'

'It's really weird.'

'So, what, you just see, like, little orange tails swimming like that, disembodied?'

'Pretty much.'

'How come it can't make that purple?'

'No idea. No one has any idea.'

'Who figured that out?'

'Me.'

An ad came on, and instead of muting I turned it up, watched a kid in pyjamas racing his toy car around a figure-eight track. The Hot Wheels logo flashed on the screen. 'Bit late for this ad, isn't it?'

'Nah, kids love him. Your dad.'

'Do they?' I raised my eyebrows at him.

'Sorry,' he said again, softer this time, and I lifted one side of my mouth. When the program resumed, there were videos of my dad as I remember him. Old. Nimble, yes, but old.

Everyone has a story of where they were when they heard, even though his death was ordinary, slipped, threw his back out, had a heart attack. I know—I overheard them in the weeks after, in cafes and shopping centres, on the plane on the way over here. On the TV at the doctors, woke up to it on the radio, their mum texted them. And mine is just as ordinary as anyone's. Sitting at home in my newly half-empty flat, my feet up on the last box of Eamon's things, thumb scrolling through Facebook, up came a Guardian article *Ruben Greenfield, dead at 74*, then the screen change. My mother calling.

I hope, if nothing else, by the time I am finished here people will be done recounting the where-were-yous.

Today it is sunny and clear for the first time in days; I won't be able to avoid working.

Jan 21st

The pattern came in the new year. The erratic behaviour of the groupers. The absence of damselfish. The rapid decline of butterfly fish. A grouping of grooming fish moving off to the same location. I saw it and I ignored it. Dismissed the signs. I thought at least that it would pass, or I convinced myself they would, although it is not a coincidence, I think, that I began to write this down when I began to interpret the cloakfish's presence.

It is not as if the information is not out there, if you want to look for it, in science journals, obscure forums. But, as Eugene hadn't asked, I hadn't felt compelled to clarify. Didn't that purple occur naturally, on the coral, on other fish—yes. But the reef is busy and you have to know what you were looking for. There is a more efficient way to find the cloakfish: equipment, both expensive and complicated, and simple and cheap—a tarp the right shade of purple can do wonders. None of this I have used on this trip. That is not why I am here, I decided. Soon I will get to go home, and Marylyn will be happy. She will forget, if she's disappointed, if she feels her collection is incomplete. I am not sure if Marylyn understands that putting a large invisible predator in the tank would immensely deplete her collection.

I'm too tired to write. I am too tired and too angry to write.

Jan 23

The water was shivering in rings. Raining, but a larger storm was coming. In scuba gear, almost done. Floating near the surface, oxygen tube out of my mouth, looking just at the coral on the surface. There was a patch of seagrass, shaggy, purple, small iridescent fish leaping from it. You can track the cloakfish, but you cannot determine where it is going to go next. Deciding not to anticipate its next move is as effective as anticipating it. When I'd noticed the signs, I'd changed direction. Although I'd been moving methodically along one stretch of reef, I chose to move to another stretch completely. The sea grass shifted—the purple disappeared and the exact nature of the reef floor became unclear. It was right there. I'd swum right up to it.

Up on the boat, looking over the edge, not at me though, at the patch of seagrass, at the cloakfish—Dad, rain pouring off his roman nose. I surfaced, too quickly, head spinning; when the water peeled back from the surface of my goggles: not Dad. Eugene on the boat, leant over, looking at me, holding a hand out. Down at the seagrass again, it's still there: the shimmer; the missing reef. Raining harder. Surface aggravated, can't see it, not anymore. Eugene's hand in mine, helping me onto the boat, into the cabin. Towelling off. Dry clothes. Twisting water out of my hair; clipping it to my head.

'See anything today?'

'Not today.'

'You sure?'

I looked out the boat window to the sky darkening to grey.

'It's raining too much now anyway.'

Jan 26

January is ending, and so is my time here. I can feel already the muscles in my back relaxing after weeks of tension. This morning I woke to a woman in a deep-blue shining dress floating at my door and thought I was again experiencing the sick beginnings of paralysis, but I found I could move; I sat up easily and she was still there. It was not a woman, simply a dress, animated by the breeze. A note from Marylyn on it: *A late Xmas present, in anticipation of the party.*

I saw the cloakfish two weeks ago, not long after I began to write all this down, when I thought I again saw my dad, then surfaced to find Eugene on the boat, but I have been caught up in the events that happened since I arrived, and time has stretched. I can feel my mind beginning to clear, though I am still dreaming in vivid hot scenes. I go walking every morning as the sun rises, Bear at my side. I go home on Sunday. The party is this Saturday, three days from now. I am looking forward to the smug look on George's face. I am looking forward to being home, in my bed, where I will stop dreaming of my dad looking down from the boat, water streaming off his face. When I surface, gone—not turned into Eugene, as he did when I saw the cloakfish in the water—just gone. Or worse, as it's getting, as the dreams become stranger, confusing my reality further, not gone, turned into Eamon, lecturing me. Sometimes before I surface even, water morphing Dad's face into his, lips moving, trying to tell me something—tell me off for something—his words an indistinct honking through the water. My own defence lost in bubbles, which in my dream glide up and crack like gunshots on the surface. That I know what I'm doing, *crack*. It isn't the worst thing, a private aquarium, *crack*. And what if it made all the difference, *crack,* for one species, even one, *crack*, what if it made a difference? *Crack*.

I will not miss these days on the boat, summoning fish from the water, only to be rehomed. Nor the sounds of the forest, the unceasing rain, eerie impossible lyrebirds. I will not miss this feeling of being constantly on edge, the tension behind my eyes, of feeling always like I should give in as I did that day it was raining in the forest and collapse in hysteria.

Today I will go out on the boat; we will stop at one spot or another. I will say it's the wrong spot, and we will move again. I will do this all day, as I did yesterday. Eugene will comply, his knowing smile on his face, and in the evening I will come back, watch strange men and women flitting through the house. I will drink champagne and stand in the corner as Marylyn circles between her guests. She will talk about her plans for conservation, about her dedication, her commitment to the marine life on the reef. And then I will go home. I will lie down on my bed, close my eyes, and the pain behind them will collapse, and maybe I will believe her.

31—

I have taken the boat. I took it as easy and simple as if I knew I always would, untied the knot in one slick pull, let my hands do the work, pushing away from the jetty, walking, swinging the wheel around, keys already in the boat like I knew they would be, like my hands knew they would be, water flicking up to damp my face, salt flecks licked from my lips, dress plastered against the front of my leg, billowing out to a tent behind me, Bear's bark booming from the sand, as the boat pulled further away from the island, woof, woof, woof, a resonating echo through the hilly tree side of the forest. I have taken the boat. What have I done, the night sky is dark and the moon sits ahead, a sliver among the stars, the island has long shrunk behind me, shrinking, shrinking as I pulled away from the jetty, the jazz and buzz from the party slipping into dark blue, what has happened, in a swig of champagne and chit-chat with Marylyn before strangers turned up, I should have asked for makeup, dear, if I had wanted any, but I did not want any, and said I was fine thank you, but it was good of me to wear the dress, dear, good of me to wear the dress, although I thought of not wearing it, I wonder what she would have done if I hadn't, but I thought best to get it all done, make her happy, go home tomorrow, well, she said, you look lovely, dear, even though I've worn no makeup and my shoes are very sensible, I look lovely, the room was lit up by new chandeliers, and the wave of water-blue refraction was not its normal neon, but a faint shadow on the floor, rippling over the skin of my feet, like veins dancing, Eugene entered in a suit the same blue as me, and we looked at one another and smiled, we couldn't help it, because we realised then what she'd done, made us like two side ornaments, but I let her have this last victory, she reached over, picked a piece of lint—real? imagined?—from his shirt collar, and she said, well, you're just gorgeous aren't you, and then spun him around and put him next to me and clasped her hands together, but then her forehead pulled tight, what about your tie, dear, and I grinned the grin of a sibling watching the golden child get reprimanded, but Eugene, he shrugged, he didn't know how to tie one, didn't really feel comfortable in it anyway, and here is a lie I have been telling you: that I do not like him, but he has been, his quiet knock in the middle of the night, the warmness of his skin, him and the dog have been two small comforts in this uncanniness, I have taken the boat, we are floating, me and the boat, we are floating off the reef, I can no longer see the island, I have stopped to write this down, I am a million hairs standing up, goosebumps running down my tail bone, a night breeze feels like it has hollowed me, guests started to arrive, and I did not know how she knew that many people, all different ages and

looks and shapes, do they all live on the island, did they come
there especially, it was her birthday party, her fiftieth, or there-
abouts, I was told, so that's what all this was for, and this young
couple, accent like rich California, *what a lovely country, wow the
beaches, as good as back home, planned on coming here for ages,*
they'd *always* wanted to come to Australia, and she just loved to
snorkel, always they'd wanted to snorkel, and they thought, well,
they looked at each other and did this upside-down, grin-teeth
clench, they thought *well* we better come while we still can, and
then the two of them laughed nervously, for all the world what
could they do about it, then she slipped her hand down to her
belly and rubbed it, and the way she rubbed it, although there
was barely a bump there, I understood she meant, before this
comes along, and not, before it is not able to be seen anymore,
although maybe she meant both, *drinking for two I am,* and
the man laughed, and he really did have two drinks, beer in one
hand, flute glass in the other, and I wondered how many times he
was going to say that tonight, there was another couple, a woman
with a lovely neck, her wife in an iridescent green dress, they
lived on the island, they said, on the other side though, where
people actually live, both laughed, weird coming out this way
this time of night, and how have I been getting on, up here with
Marylyn, and the two of them they looked at me like they knew
exactly what I've been doing here, how I've been handling here,
all this time, and there were so many people in that room, its
fullest self, full of light and people, men and women, waiters in
black and white ironed attire, my age, a little younger, students,
how did she get a whole catering company out there, both of the
women were tall, and the one in the green dress had hair like

fresh vines at the start of spring, coiled and falling to her shoulders, and I thought, she looks like Mother Nature, I thought, and she looked at me like she understood everything I'd done, and for a second I felt the complete relief of a child being told they are not a bad person, that I am trying my best, and we all make mistakes, but then the other woman frowned, a deep frown and hissed, what the fuck is he doing here, and her wife tried to calm her, I looked where she was looking and I see a man with a grey rim of hair and a shiny bald patch on the other side of the room, I felt something like familiarity, my mind grasping the contours of something but not its contents, and, as I was trying to fill this gap, this absence, I began to think maybe he was a politician, but then no, he's not a politician, I've just confused him with one, then the woman hissed again, what the fuck is he doing here, and it looked like she was about to yell, and at once I understood why, my hands became hot, my hands always become hot when I am full of dread, although right now I can't feel them, can barely feel my hands at all, but then my hands were hot so very hot because the hole in my head became three dimensional, took on shade and nuance, and I recognised the man, the man over there in the corner, who had made his fortune on coal, and the woman who looked very upset, I thought maybe she was about to yell something, when her wife grabbed her arm and whispered in her ear, and the woman, the woman looked very distressed, and then looked down at her feet, as if she didn't know how she got there, as if she had been tricked into being there, but then there was purple, purple Marylyn in her dress before us, some strange exotic feathers poking out the top of her head, and she said, *hello my lovelies,* and I knew then it was just the drink, and that woman was not Mother Nature and she did not forgive me, and if I have believed that I am *just trying my best, just getting on with business,* it is a veneer, underneath my insides are eaten through, like termites through soft pine, full of rotting, don't worry, Eamon, I know, and how could I possibly keep on with this fish, with this hobbyist fish, when the reef is disintegrating around me, he wanted to know, how could I do it, and I couldn't answer at the time, but now I know it's because my insides are just like the reef, bleaching, I am also losing my colour, becoming full of holes, a tray of spring rolls, saffron curled up like pubic hair on top passed under my nose, I took one, moving around the room, strangers passed their hands on my shoulder, said what a magnificent collection, and I did see George for a second, and he smiled at me, said, no cloakfish I see, I think I owe him some money, and I said that sounds unlike me, making a bet, and he said, did it now, we'll have to see about that love, and I mumbled and moved away from him just as Marylyn, her hands above her head weaving through the crowd, toward a little—I almost laughed—podium set up in front of the tank, facing the crowd and smiling, her lipstick purple, she moved up toward the podium, but she stopped and touched the elbow of a guest standing there and they both embraced, and when she finally did get up on the podium, and the crowd started shushing each other, and someone said alright now, settle down, her lipstick was a dark slash of purple, no, not a slash, a ribbon, a zipper opening, she said thank you, thank you all for coming, especially, thank you to my husband, Henry, for his loving support, and then of course, of course she did, she motioned to the man with the bald patch in the suit who raised his glass to polite applause, and then he cleared his throat, he said you're welcome darling, and then and then he said, *and then he said, your hobby is my carbon offset!* and the men around him laughed they laughed, and so did Marylyn, before she shushed the crowd and thank you all, she said, thank you all for coming, then she put her arms out, put her arms out again, and then the tank glass behind her began to wobble, but it wasn't the glass, but the water that began to distort in this strange fisheye, and the colours of the crowd shifted into the water behind her, phased into a round image behind her, right in the middle of window, like a distorted mirror, and the crowd was silent now, then an audible oooh, and she seemed satisfied that she'd brought this pleasure to the crowd, until she realised they were not looking at her, but just behind her, and she turned comically, with her arms still outstretched toward the audience, swivelled her neck around, but the image of the crowd reflected back at them was off, where she was in the middle was wrong, her purple dress was not in it, instead it was like the image could not come into focus, could not complete itself, and the distortion of the water moved again and my stomach with it, the bottom of the cloakfish reflecting the crowd back to us, trying to blend not into the water, but with its belly on the glass, into the crowd, and I turned to look around the room at faces with hanging jaws, and I saw Eugene looking at me with this small smile, like he was sorry, but what did I expect, and I was leaving, I was running, running out the door, and through another door, to the corridor and another, so many ways to be lost in that house, to run around in its depths forever, but then I was outside, and down into the cabin for my bag and then out, out again through to the track in the forest, Bear barked once in greeting and when I ran past him he kept barking and followed me down the slope, down through the forest to the boat, on the boat I sit now writing this and realise what I have done, when I finish this I will turn around, I will turn the engine on, and turn around and go back to the island, I will wait until the party is over, I will hike up my dress and pull out the tank, the long flat tank with the trolley Eugene uses, must have used, on some other jetty to drive the fish to the house, I will push that tank up that hill, the water slopping out and wetting me further, Bear will be waiting for me barking at all the commotion, or he will be silent and absent and scared, John will be taking the guests to their cars, arranging transport, I will rage my way back up that hill with the tank on the trolley, up to that house, I will stop in her room and I will rip purple from her hangings, rip purple bed sheets, pillow cases from their places, and in some miracle they will almost all be the right shade, and I will march my way up those stairs, I will find a way into the tank, and I will plunge myself into that cold water, but to me the water will be warm and soothing, it will be rejuvenating, and I will cover the bottom with purple and I will find that fish, or that fish will find me and take me with it to the bottom and I will wrestle it, and I will rip that fish from its new home and only when I have slipped it into the long flat tank and taken it all the way back down the hill, balanced it as its weight pulls it rolling down ahead of me, me running to catch up, only when my dress has ripped and clung to my body and my chest is heaving in the exhaustion of not helping when I should have, and helping where I don't need to, only when the fish, scared and exhausted, has slipped back and dissolved into the reef, only when I have saved it from becoming something else, only when I have realised it was not me, it was never me, that was the cloakfish, but I will not let them take it from me, Marylyn or that man, I will not let them embody it, only then will I know I have done something right, and when I sleep tonight, for once I will not dream of my father.

Yes, when I finish writing this, that is what I will do.

Or—maybe I will turn the engine back on, keep the boat turned toward the moon and drive onward, laughing, and crying, and laughing, the presence of him, my dad, in his youth, I can feel him now, putting his feet up on the back of the boat, and the two of us, my father and me, will keep driving off into the night, until the fuel gauge runs low, and the boat stutters to a halt. Then, maybe, I will slip myself off into the water, and blend seamlessly into the deep blue.

Notes on These Stories

A version of 'Meat Alternatives for the Motherland: A Review' appeared in *Meanjin*. A version of 'Orchestra of Animals' appeared in the Kill Your Darlings Anthology *New Australian Fiction 2020*. 'Constellation in the Left Eye' appeared in *Overland*. A version of 'Preparation' was longlisted for the 2020 Peter Carey Prize, and appeared in *Going Down Swinging*. 'Fertile Soil' was Pacific region winner of the 2021 Commonwealth Short Story Prize, and appeared in *Granta*.

Acknowledgements

Thank you to:
All the brilliant, intelligent, ridiculous, frustrating women
I know. My parents: Dad, Mum—for both her parental and
editorial advice, and to who this book is rightfully dedicated—and Glenn. Myles McGuire and Kate Elkington, some
of the first readers of this book, whose advice was invaluable.
Dr Emily Barber for her work on some of the earlier stories.
Jenny Odell and her people at Frances Goldin Literary Agency
for permission rights to *All the People in on Pier 39*. The editors
of the journals and anthologies where some of these stories
first appeared, and the judges of the 2021 Commonwealth
Short Story Prize. Kat, Maddy, Ben, Eilish, Michaela, Alex,
and Myles, for their companionship, warmth and wit, and
all the other friends, teachers, and pets who enriched my life
over the years. My agent Caitlan Cooper-Trent for her hard work
and support. My copy editor Meredith Rose. Alissa Dinallo for

her beautiful cover design. Katherine Ring for her sharp eye. My publisher Ben Ball, who is responsible for making this book the best version of itself, and to who I am deeply grateful for his insight, grace, and guidance. My cat Eva. And of course Tyler, my love.